Hated
YOU THEN

LOVE HURTS BOOK 1

WALL STREET JOURNAL AND USA TODAY BESTSELLING AUTHOR

M. ROBINSON

xo

M. Robinson
WALL STREET JOURNAL & USA TODAY BESTSELLING AUTHOR
QUEEN OF ANGST

www.authormrobinson.com

Dedication

For Leeann Van Rensburg & Jamie Guellar

Thank you for always helping wherever is needed. You ladies are rock stars.

Acknowledgments

And so it begins…

Cover & Graphic Designer/ Proofreader/Personal Assistant/Heather Moss: My Yoda. Where do I start, where do I finish? After almost five years of you being my right-hand woman, there isn't much I haven't already said to you at some point. Usually in these acknowledgments. Thank you for everything! I am always impressed with your willingness to help me in any situation. You handle whatever task I throw your way with no questions asked. You have no idea how grateful I am to have you in my life, both professionally and personally. Your hard work, determination, and work ethic never goes unnoticed. I just want you to know that you're deeply appreciated, and I can't thank you enough for all you do.

Editor/Erin Noelle: You have been my editor for my last ten books and your suggestions always bring more life to my stories. Thank you for loving my babies the way you do.

Publicist/Danielle Sanchez: I can't thank you enough for the knowledge you bring to my brand. Wildfire Marketing Solutions is amazing. I'm so lucky to have you as my publicist.

Bloggers/Bookstagramers: Most of you have been with me since I started my writing career over six years ago. I can't thank you enough for always supporting me every way you can. I appreciate and love you so much. I couldn't do this without you. You're real MVP's!

My VIPS/Readers: I. Love. You. From the bottom of my heart, thank you!!! For everything.

Photographer: Rafagcatala
Cover Model: Adrian Pedraja
TBC Trailers: Cinematic Trailer

Teasers & Promo: Lori Loves Book Jackson, Kinky Girls Book Obsessions, Leeann Van Rensburg, Emma Louise

Paperback & Ebook Formatter: V. Fryer, Formats by Vicki

My VIP Reader Group Admins: Lily Garcia, Emma Louise, Jennifer Pon, Jessica Laws, Louisa Brandenburger, Michelle Chambers, Nicole Erard

Alphas & Betas: Michelle Tan, Tammy McGowan, Michele Henderson McMullen, Carrie Waltenbaugh, Mary Jo Toth, Ella Gram, Tricia Bartley, Patti Correa, Maria Naylet, Deborah E Shipuleski, Kaye Blanchard, Georgina Marie Kerslake, Ashley Reynolds, Chasidy Renee, Danielle Renee, Marci Antoinette Gant, Dee Renee Hudson, Misty Horn, Nohely Clark, Ashley Singer-Falkner, Mary Sittu-Kern, Sanne Heremans, Kris Carlile, Elena Reyes

Street Team, Good Ol' Girls: Tracey Wilson-Vuolo, Melinda Parker, Amanda Roden, Terri Handschumacher, Nysa Bookish, Darlene Pollard, Ashley Sledge, Wendy Livingstone, Donna Fernandez, Corie Olson, Beverly Gordon, Ann B. Goubert, Keshia Craft, Yvette Lynch, Vanessa Reyes, Amy Coury, Shawna Kolczynski, Christin Yates Herbert, Nysa Bookish Read, Sarah Polglaze, Darlene S Pollard, Chantel Curry, Jill Bourne, Tara Horowitch, Rhonda Ziglar, Michelle Chambers, Lily Jameson, Paula DeBoer, Jessica Laws, Nicole Erard, Marci Antoinette Gant

VIP Reader Group Hype Girls: Melinda Parker, Terri Handschumacher, Darlene Pollard, Dawn Walsh, Angela Hart, Oindrilla Sarkar, Vanessa Reyes, Darlene S Pollard, Chantel Curry, Paula DeBoer

Prologue

Harley

Now

Two plus signs.
A smiley face.
One plus sign.
Two pink lines.
One pink line.
And then the word…
Pregnant.
Clear as day for me to read. I took six different pregnancy tests, and they all gave me the same exact result.
Never did I imagine this was where I would be at twenty years old.
Knocked up.
With child.
Bun in the oven.
Bastard.
How was I going to tell my family?
My daddy?
Or worse…
The father.
I was having a baby with the man I least expected.
Because you see, I hated him.
He hated me.

We hated each other.

Except after everything we'd gone through, done to each other, been through together. Deep in my heart, my soul, my entire being…

I loved him.

Chapter One

Harley

Then: Six years old

My first word was *fuck*.

But only cuz my daddy said it all the time.

"Harley, are you listening to me?" Momma asked, shuttin' the refrigerator door with a thud.

I nodded, but I wasn't listenin' at all. I just kept drawin' a picture of my daddy in the unicorn notebook in front of me. Thinkin' about him and not that butthole, Jackson Pierce.

My daddy was my everythin'.

Most little kids would say their daddies were their heroes, but my daddy really was a hero. I ain't even playin'. He saved my momma's life, like for real, for real. Daddy was the reason her heart was still beatin'.

Cuz his blood ran through her veins when he saved her life with a transfusion.

And that wasn't the only time Daddy saved Momma.

He rescued her a lot, a lot. Like five times from all the bad guys tryin' to steal her away from him.

Includin' my Uncle Noah.

I know… crazy, right?

But Daddy says Momma saved him from himself, whatever that meant.

"Young lady, this behavior needs to stop. How many times have I told you—"

"Umm hmm," I hummed, completely ignorin' her.

My daddy was also a hero of war, which was like way better than Jackson's doctor daddy anyway. He was a soldier for our country and brought the flag home. It was in the clubhouse in his office, along with all his other medals. He had lots of them cuz he was a real hero, not just a pretend one.

My baby brother Owen was even named after Daddy's military brother who died in battle. Daddy said he wanted his memory to live on forever and ever, so Owen carries a very special name.

Like me.

Harley.

Daddy named me after his favorite thing in the universe besides Momma, his bike.

Anyone who said Harleys weren't the best piece of machinery known to man could kiss Daddy's ass. His words, not mine. I wasn't allowed to cuss. It always got me in a whole lot of trouble.

Just like Jackson did.

Luke was our middle brother. He was named after Daddy's baby brother who died when he was little. I was the oldest, so that meant I'd heard all the stories of Momma and Daddy's lives so many times I knew them by heart. Daddy was the best bedtime storyteller, ever. I told all my friends their stories, even though Momma said I couldn't talk 'bout those things.

I didn't listen to her…

I talked 'bout them anyway, cuz my daddy was the best daddy in all the world, and everyone needed to know it.

Especially *Jackson Pierce.*

"Harley, have you heard a word I said?" she questioned again.

"Yep," I replied, poppin' my *p*.

I still wasn't listenin'. I knew what she was gonna say. It was always the same thing.

"Harley, you can't hit Jackson."

"Harley, why did you hit Jackson?"

"Harley, you have to stop hitting Jackson."

And what she said the most…

"Harley, you're grounded."

This wasn't the first or the last time I'd be in trouble cuz of fart-breath Jackson Pierce.

"Then what did I say?" Momma asked, stoppin' in front of me, shakin' her head.

"That Jackson Pierce is a stupid, ugly-faced booger."

"Harley Jameson!"

He is!

Jackson was always sayin' his daddy was better than mine, cuz his daddy saved lives.

Well, duh, that's what doctors do.

It wasn't that I didn't think Jackson's daddy was awesome. He was, but he wasn't *more* awesome than mine.

Why couldn't they be the same level of awesomeness?

Whatever.

Everyone said Jackson was the golden child, cuz he was good at everythin'...

Barf.

He wasn't as good as me, cuz I was way better than him.

At anythin'and everythin'.

Always.

And I made sure he knew that every chance I got, even if it got me grounded, forever. He needed to know he could kiss my butt, and I made sure he never forgot.

I ignored him for the most part. At least I tried to, but he was always gettin' me in trouble with his stupid mouth. Momma said to pretend like he wasn't there, but when I did, he was just a bigger bully with his huge reindeer ears and nose.

Rudolph The Red-Nosed Reindeer.

Jackson never stopped either. Sometimes he would pretend to be nice when adults were around, but he was always a turd.

A big fat one.

Sayin' he was better than me, tryin' to boss me around. Kickin', pushin', puttin' me in headlocks, or holdin' me down on the ground until I said or did what he wanted.

So annoyin'...

I never gave in, ever.

And I never would.

Besides, all I had to do when he was pickin' on me was what my daddy said to do.

So, I did.

"My daddy says if boys bother me to kick 'em where the sun don't shine," I told Jackson for the first time.

"What's that?"

I didn't wait to explain before kickin' him in the nuts.

He fell to the ground, hurtin'. "What the heck, Harley?!"

"What?" I shrugged. "I was just showin' ya what you asked."

"Just wait! I'm gonna knock you into next week!"

"Good! Then I won't havta' see your ugly face that makes me wanna barf!"

And the next day, he did just that… Never did I imagine he would take it as far as he did.

Never.

Ever.

Under no circumstances.

I gasped. Screamin', "Not my limited-edition Christmas Barbie!" Knowin' who was behind this.

I ran across my room, leapin' over my bed to get to her. Carefully takin' her headless body off the string that was around her neck. Straightening her red sparklin' gown, feelin' like I got punched in my tummy.

When I looked up, there the murderer was, leanin' against the doorway with his arms crossed over his chest. An evil look takin' over his face.

One you'd see in 'R' rated movies.

"Jackson Pierce, you are rotten to the core! What did Barbie ever do to you to deserve this?!"

"You had my nuts hurting all day, Harley!"

"I hate you and your nuts!" I didn't wait again, I tackled him to the ground into the hallway.

"Get off me, you Gremlin!"

"Never, you asshole!"

"Harley Jameson!" Momma yelled in that really, really angry voice. The one she only used when I was in lots and lots of trouble.

I didn't get off him until she pulled me away, and then I got grounded for life, again.

Nothin' new.

"Harley, this has to stop," Momma stressed, pullin' me away from my memory.

"Ugh!" I stomped my foot. "I don't wanna do this, Momma! I hate him! I don't wanna pretend like I don't hate him!"

"Oh, it's perfectly clear you hate him, young lady. I think you've hated him since the day you were born."

14

"I have. He sucks big, huge donkey balls."

"Harley! You can't talk like that."

"Momma, if you heard half of the things he's said to me, you would think he sucks, too."

"I have heard the things he says to you, Harley. It's not like you two try to hide your hatred for each other. It's well known to everyone in town how much you can't stand one another. Why do you think you're not allowed on the opposite teams at school anymore, young lady? Remember you hit Jackson with a baseball bat last year?"

"It wasn't even that hard."

"Harley, you knocked him out for ten seconds."

"He was wearin' a helmet, and he woke back up." I shook my head. "He was fine. And I only hit him cuz he hit me first."

"You got hit with a foul ball."

"That he was pitchin'!"

"Harley, enough! You kicked him in the nuts, *again*. For the fifth time this month."

"He blocked a few!"

"Only after the first time you kicked him."

"That's only cuz he said I couldn't jump as high as he could off the swings, when he *knows* I can. I'm the highest jumper in the first grade."

Why did Jackson have to try and beat me at everythin'?

Why was he so ugly it hurt my eyes to look at him? And make me want to barf when he was around?

I didn't know.

"And what did I say about using your words?"

I scratched my head. "But Daddy says—"

"Harley, I didn't ask you what your father said, I asked you what *I* said."

Looking down at the ground, I whispered, "To use my words instead of my fists."

"That's ri—"

I couldn't hold it in any longer. "But Daddy says sometimes fists speak louder than words."

"Damn straight, baby girl," Daddy stated, walking into the kitchen.

"Creed!" Momma turned, yelling at him like always. Making me giggle.

Momma was always yelling at him for the stuff that came out of his mouth, cuz my daddy was awesome and always did and said what

15

he wanted.

He cussed.

A lot, a lot.

Daddy had a potty mouth, and I had a potty mouth cuz of him.

I was always gettin' yelled at by adults to watch my language. Little girls were supposed to be polite and delicate and turn into beautiful young ladies.

Bigger barf.

Well, I didn't wanna be like that.

I just wanted to be myself.

Harley Jameson.

The biker princess of the baddest, scariest, meanest biker of them all. Prez of the End of the Road motorcycle club. Creed Jameson.

My daddy.

Chapter Two

Harley

Daddy came from a really super long line of bikers. Like a list of hundreds and hundreds of years long. Biker blood ran through my veins like it did my momma's cuz Daddy made me with his seed. He planted me in Momma's tummy with his water hose.

That was how babies were made.

By gardenin'.

Daddy said I wasn't allowed to garden until I was fifty years old. It was okay, cuz I didn't wanna garden anyway. Boys were stupid.

Except for my very best friend in the whole wide world, Cash McGraw. But I still didn't wanna garden with him.

Momma said Cash had been my best friend since the day I was born. He hated Jackson, too. Not as much as I hated him. No one hated him as much as I did, but Jackson hated Cash, too. They didn't like each other cuz Cash knew I was better than Jackson and always stuck up for me. Even though I didn't need him to, I could kick Jackson's butt, and I showed Cash…

All. The. Time.

I still remember a few years ago when Jackson said his willy was bigger than Cash's willy. It all started when Cash ran out of the bathroom naked at one of his parents' parties cuz the lights went out in his house from the thunderstorm.

"Cash," I breathed out, looking at him. *"What's that?"*

"What?" he replied.

I nodded to the stuffed animal coverin' his privates, and he looked down at what I was starin' at.

"Oh, that's just Nemo. Ya know, from Finding Nemo.*"*

"No, silly, behind Nemo."

"Oh..." He shrugged. "That's just my willy. One day it will be as big as my dad's."

The whole room busted out laughin', besides Daddy. He picked me up and threw me over his shoulder like a sack of potatoes, grumblin' somethin' 'bout puttin' little shits to ground.

But on the way out of the room, I heard Jackson shout, "Oh, mine's already as big as my dad's!"

And the room exploded into more laughter.

Til' this day, I didn't know if what they said was true or not. It probably wasn't for Jackson, cuz I kicked him in the nuts a lot and I never felt his willy. Not that I wanted to.

Yuck.

One of my favorite things to do with Cash was to close my eyes and dance around to his music. I felt the songs in my heart and really deep in my bones. Like super deep, almost touchin' my insides.

Cash always had his guitar on him, singin' and playin' music for me. He was gonna be super famous one day and buy me a pony I was gonna name Buttercup. Cash even made me a song with a bluesy beat he sang and played for me all the time. Cash could play the blues better than anyone on this entire planet and that was a lot of people.

His daddy, Dylan McGraw, was a detective in North Carolina and one of the good ol' boys like my papaw, Lucas Ryder. Cash never said his daddy was better than mine like Jackson did. Our daddies were tied for awesomeness.

My other best friend was a girl, like me, and her name was Shiloh Foster. Shiloh was my cousin cuz her momma was my Aunt Lily, who was my pawpaw's sister. Her dad, Uncle Jacob, was a lawyer for super important people, and he was one of the good ol' boys, too.

Everyone always called us the good ol' kids cuz our daddies were the best. They were all tied in awesomeness. There were other good ol' kids our age, like Bentley Taylor. His daddy was Austin Taylor, who owned the greatest tattoo shop in North Carolina.

 Bentley was my friend too, but not my best friend. All the other kids were older than us by a lot, especially my Uncle Mason and Giselle, who was Cash's older sister. They were the oldest.

I once heard my pawpaw say the good ol' boys were only good for screwin'. Which made sense, cuz he was a contractor and screwed a lot of things.

Shiloh was actually the secretary of our Hate Jackson Pierce Club, and Cash was the Vice Prez. I, of course, was the President.

We had church like Daddy did with his club, where we talked about how much he sucked.

"Hey, baby," Daddy said, kissin' me on the tip of my nose like he did every day when he got home from work.

"Hi, Daddy."

"How's my girl?"

"Eh." I shrugged. "Ain't as happy as a pig in poop."

Daddy smiled. "Now we can't have that, yeah?"

"Creed, she's in trouble at school, again. This is the fifth time this month."

"Better than last month."

I smiled.

See, Daddy gets me.

"Creed... I'm the one having to answer to her teacher and principal."

"That's on you, Pippin. I'd gladly go tell that motherfuc—"

I smiled again, wider that time. Daddy almost said the really, really bad word that got him in trouble too. It must be a doozy since everyone always got in trouble for sayin' it.

Anytime I cussed, it got me grounded, forever, again. But it wasn't my fault. I was around bikers my whole entire life, and that was a really long time. Those were the words they used, bad ones.

Daddy's younger brother, Uncle Noah, wasn't any better with his potty mouth. It was just how us Jamesons were made.

Bad ass mothafuckas.

If Momma heard me say that, it would get me grounded forever again, but it was the truth. That was what they said all the time. I didn't know what those words meant either, but it still sounded really cool like "asshole".

"My baby girl is just defendin' herself from the little shit, Mia."

I nodded really, really fast so Momma could see how true that was.

"Really? Then explain how *she* is the one who keeps trying to kick him in the nuts, Creed?"

Daddy looked at me. "Why did you try to take him down again, baby?"

"Cuz he made me, Daddy."

"See, Pippin, he made her."

19

He'd called Momma "Pippin" since she was little like me. It was after Pippi Longstocking, the coolest girl of them all.

Momma rolled her eyes at him before looking at me. "How did he make you, Harley?"

"Cuz he was tellin' Becky I couldn't jump off the swing as high as him."

Daddy grinned. "So, he was pickin' on you?"

"Yes."

"Good girl."

"CREED!"

"What, babe?"

"Don't '*what babe*' me. She needs to learn violence isn't the answer to dealing with Jackson. You encourage her behavior."

"They're kids. She's just showin' him who's boss."

I nodded again, faster.

"Creed, this isn't your MC world. It's elementary school, and she needs to learn right from wrong."

"I know right from wrong, Momma. Just sometimes wrong feels right." I smiled, showing her my pearly whites while Daddy tried to hide his smile.

"*Creed...*"

"I didn't say a word."

Daddy always spoke with his eyes and face, and right now, he was in trouble for it.

Sorry, Daddy.

"Harley, your father and I need to have a word."

People were always havin' a word in my life where lots and lots of bad ones were used. Especially at the clubhouse. I guess havin' a word meant cussin'. I wasn't allowed to have words, cuz I was still little. But when I got bigger, I'd use all the words I already knew.

Which was a lot.

Until then, I'd just use them on Jackson 'Asshole' Pierce.

"When I get back, these letters to Jackson, his mom, and your teacher better be finished. Do you understand me, young lady?"

"Mmm hmm."

"*Harley...*" she said my name in the same voice she did Daddy's.

"Yes, I understand."

"Good."

"But, Momma." I crossed my arms. "What words am I allowed to use, since you already crossed out all the ones I used?"

20

She sighed, handing me back the letter I'd written to Jackson.

"Go ahead, read it out loud to your father."

"But, Momma, you crossed out all of my words."

"You can still read through them, Harley."

"Fine." I took a long breath and started reading.

"Dear Jackson Butthole Pierce,

I really hate u and your stupid face more than I did yesterday. I hope u fall off your bed and land on your Rudolph nose that makes me wanna puke every time I look at u. And then I hope u get runned over by a bus on the way to schol so I don't havta' to see ya again and u can't ever get me in trouble no more.

I hate u.

U suck.

Not love, Harley."

I peeked up at them through my lashes.

"Keep going," she ordered in the same tone from before.

I took another long breath. **"P.S. I heard u r adopted and your mom really found u in the garbage outside of Memaw's restaurant."**

"Keep going…"

I rolled my eyes. **"I'm not sorry I kicked you in the nuts again cuz u deserved it for bein' a stupid bully asshole who scares my fish with your butthole face."**

I shrugged, peeking up at them again. "You said to tell him how I felt. I did what you asked, and now I'm in trouble."

"Harley, you were in trouble before you wrote the letter that you will be writing again."

"I'm only in trouble cuz Jackson, Momma. Why ain't he in trouble too? You always take his side."

"Oh, he's in trouble, Harley. He's writing you a letter as well."

"Yeah, it'll prolly be bombed with his farts. *Gross.*"

"Baby, do as your momma says, and I'll take you for a ride later."

Going on rides with Daddy on his motorcycle was one of my favorite things to do.

"Okay, Daddy."

"Creed, how is that going to teach her any—"

He pulled Momma into a kiss, making me giggle. That was Daddy's go-to move when he was in trouble, cuz Momma loved his kisses like she loved mine.

"Reel it in, babe. Ya feel me?" he said, grinning.

Momma whispered something in his ear that made him laugh

21

before smacking him on the chest, but Daddy didn't move at all.

He never did.

Cuz he was the boss.

One day I was gonna marry a man just like my daddy, cuz he was the best man of them all.

Little did I know…

How true that was.

Chapter Three

Jackson

Then: Seven years old

"Jackson Pierce, do you have your letter for Harley?" Mom asked in the same tone she'd been using all weekend.

The one that meant I was still in a buttload of trouble because of none other than Gremlin face, Harley Jameson. She looked just like a Gremlin, and not the cute one, Gizmo. The ugly messed up one, Stripe. Her lips were too big for her face and so were her huge blue eyes. She acted like him too. Always so violent, making snarling noises when she was angry, thinking she was the boss of me. She wasn't the leader.

Ever.

I was.

Always.

I tried ignoring the disappointed look on my mom's face as she stared at me through the rearview mirror in our SUV. I hated that look, it made my insides hurt, but not even her upset expression stopped me from fighting with dumbass Harley.

I couldn't tell you how or when our hatred for each other started. It seemed like it was always there from what everyone had told us. There was something about her stupid face and loud mouth that just got to me.

All. The. Time.

There was no controlling the effect she always had on me.

I. Hated. Her.

More than I hated the vegetables my mom was always trying to make me eat. I never did. I just pretended and when she wasn't looking, I'd spit them in my napkin and save them for later to use on the nut-kicker.

There was nothing better in all the world than to hold her down and stuff them into her mouth.

"Jackson! Get off me!" she shouted the last time this happened.

"Fat chance, baby girl."

She hated being called that by anyone other than her daddy.

"I'm not a baby girl!"

I grabbed her hand and used it to slap her own face around. "Harley, stop hitting yourself."

"Oh my God! Just wait—"

Right when her mouth was wide enough, I stuffed my dried-up broccoli that smelled like rotten eggs in it, and she went crazy. Moving her body every way she could, which wasn't much, because she was a pee wee girl and I was still sitting on top of her.

She was about to spit them out, but I covered her mouth so she couldn't.

"Swallow, you butt munch."

She screamed through my hand.

"I put those little green trees on my nuts, Harley, since you love kicking them so much. How do they feel in your mouth?"

Her eyes widened. I didn't really do that, but she didn't have to know I was lying.

"Jackson, are you listening to me?"

"Mmm hmm," I mumbled, looking out the window with my ear buds in.

"Jackson..."

"Yes, I have it."

"The good letter?"

"Maybe."

"Jackson Pierce," she said in a sterner tone. The one that meant I was walking a thin line of patience with her.

It didn't matter. I was already grounded again. Because of *her*.

"Well you made me rewrite it ten times. I'm not sure which is the good letter anymore."

"Jackson, watch your tone with your mother," Dad warned, looking at me through the same mirror.

Adults could always have a tone, but when I had one…

I got in trouble, always.

24

I didn't reply.

I knew better.

My dad was cool, but I knew what lines I couldn't cross with him. And disrespecting my mom was number one on that list. Don't get me wrong, my parents were awesome, especially my dad. He was way better than Harley's dad, and I reminded her of that all the time.

He was Doctor Aiden Pierce, Chief of Surgery at Dosher Memorial Hospital in Southport. He saved lives every single day, while hers used to put them to ground. That was biker slang for shooting bitches in the face. Her dad was badass, I'll give her that, but he wasn't better than mine.

No one's was.

"I'd like to see the apology letter before you hand it to Harley," Mom stated, bringing my eyes back to her.

"I still don't understand why *I* had to write her a letter. *She* kicked *me* in the nuts, remember?"

"*She* only kicked *you* because *you* provoked *her*," Jagger added. Making me roll my eyes at my younger brother, who was sitting in the backseat next to me.

"Whose side are you on?" I punched him.

He punched me back.

"Boys! Don't start!" Mom shouted at us. "I will turn this car around and take you both home so fast. Do you understand me?"

"Yes, ma'am," we grumbled.

My bro and I got along for the most part, except when it came to Harley. He liked her for some reason, and she didn't even have boobs.

"Good. Where is the letter, Jackson?"

I ignored Mom's question, replying, "She can't jump as high as me off the swings. How is that provoking her?"

"Do not play innocent, young man. You pick on her every chance you get."

"That's cuz she's asking for it every time she opens her mouth on her stupid face."

"Jackson!"

"What?!" I tore off my ear buds. "You act like it's always me. It's not. She starts it half the time. My nuts are probably broken with how many times she's kicked them, but does anyone care about my balls? Nope!"

"Jackson Pierce, you cannot talk like that! You're grounded!"

"I'm already grounded!"

25

"Then you're grounded some more!"

I wasn't allowed to cuss, but when you heard something all the time, it was kind of hard not to repeat it. Harley's mouth was worse than mine though. We grew up around a family full of foul-mouthed bikers, and it was just how they talked.

Plus, my dad wasn't any better. My parents grew up in the system pretty much their whole life, meaning they'd seen some shit. I didn't believe in the mushy girly crap my mom made me watch with her, but my parents were real life soulmates. They'd known each other since they were kids, they were all each other had. My dad worked his ass off to give her the life she deserved.

They deserved.

He was my role model, my hero, a man to be respected. I never had to ask for anything, no one did. He made sure of it.

Which was one of the reasons my mom took her role as a stay-at-home mom so seriously, making me act, think, and talk older than I really was. Jagger and I were smart, and I could do anything and everything before Harley Jameson ever could. Of course, I never let her live it down.

Our families were close because of Harley's Uncle Noah. Her old man's younger brother was like my old man's firstborn. He wasn't my biological brother, but you wouldn't ever think that. Noah was always there for me, and I knew I could count on him.

No matter what.

My dad took on the role of being a father figure to Noah since he was fifteen years old. Replacing his piece of shit dad, who wasn't a good man.

Or a good father.

He met Noah in the emergency room, when he was the on-call doctor during his residency at Dosher Memorial. Noah's mother was a drunk, and his old man was an asshole Prez of a 1% MC club, which meant the Jameson brothers—her dad and uncle—used to be trouble with a capital T.

My dad took Noah under his wing, always seeing things in people most would run away from. But not my dad, he was someone to look up to.

In everything.

We'd heard the story hundreds of times, and still every time I heard it, I couldn't imagine Harley's grandmother, Diane, being anything but the loving, caring woman she was now. I guess back in the day that wasn't the case.

Now all this was a long ass time ago, before any of us were born.

I never understood how dumbass Harley could have such a badass family and she was…

Not.

I reminded her of that when I tried to make her cry. It got her all peeved, and I loved every second of it. It made up for all the times I couldn't get her to shed a tear. And trust me, I tried.

A lot.

The Gremlin was made of freaking stone. I couldn't for the life of me get her to break down. Even the time she broke her leg because of me.

A year ago I dared her to jump off the roof of the clubhouse into the pool. I didn't think she'd actually do it.

But she did.

And holy shit was I in trouble.

Still the Gremlin did not cry. Instead, she beat me with her crutches when my mom made me give her flowers and apologize.

It didn't matter what I said or did, tears never spilled out. Only pushing me harder to get them to.

One day I'd make it happen, and it would be the best freaking feeling in the world.

Until then…

I'd keep trying.

.

Chapter Four

Jackson

Out of nowhere, the car stopped and it took me a second to realize where we were.

"Jackson," Dad said, turning around with a stern look on his face, pulling me away from my thoughts. "Enough."

We were on our way to the End of the Road clubhouse for the Jameson's weekly barbeque.

The MC hosted the family event every Sunday, rain or shine. Where the parents would bs about how great their kids were, and the kids would see how much trouble they could get in without getting caught.

I usually loved Sundays, being around a bunch of bikers who treated me like I was one of them. It was always the highlight of my week, except for football.

I'd been playing football ever since I could remember. Everyone always said I had one hell of an arm, so they made an exception to let me play for our city league. I was the youngest player at seven, but I was still the most valuable player.

Quarterback.

The best part of being MVP were the cheerleaders. They didn't know I wasn't twelve yet, and I didn't tell them otherwise. Just one of the perks of being a football star meant I was popular in all the nearby school districts. Everyone knew who I was…

And I meant everyone.

Football was life in our small beach town and scouts were already looking at me for college and I was only in the second grade.

I was kind of a big deal around these parts.

Neither the bikers nor the coaches gave a shit if I cussed, talked about all the girls that liked me, or even when I needed to fix my junk in public.

Sometimes it was all three at once, and no one said a word about it.

It was guy stuff.

At the clubhouse, we'd have so much fun blowing shit up, shooting rifles, looking for trouble in the woods. Which dumbass, annoying, loud-mouth Harley Jameson always thought she could be part of.

"Why are we at the Gremlin's house instead of the clubhouse?"

"Jagger, can you ride with Harley's parents? Luke's waiting for you," Mom said to him while she turned and looked at me. "Harley's mother and I thought it would be a good idea if we made the two of you spend some quality time together."

Before I could say something about the stupidest idea ever, Jagger opened the door and got out.

"Traitor!" I shouted as he shut the door behind him.

Jagger and Harley's younger brother Luke were complete opposites. Luke was the firstborn son of a biker Prez, and Jagger was the son of a surgeon, but it never stopped them from being friends.

I watched him get into their truck as Harley stepped out, all while Mom went on about something.

"Jackson, are you listening to me?" she asked.

"Uh huh." I wasn't listening at all. I was too busy watching dipstick walk over to our SUV.

Why does she always dress like she put her clothes on in the dark?

She called herself a "fashionista", whatever that meant. To me, she looked like a ballerina who pooped out a unicorn. She was wearing a bright pink shirt, rainbow tutu, red heart leggings, and glittered purple Chucks.

She always wore Converse sneakers. She was a girly-girl who acted like a boy. Every time I reminded her of that, she'd hit me. Still didn't make any damn sense.

There were sparkly cat ears on her head and a bazillion different colored bracelets on her arms that went from her wrists almost to her elbows. A mermaid backpack was slung over her right shoulder with a pink furry purse, that looked like a dead animal, hanging from the other one.

29

I sat there staring at the walking disaster coming toward me, shaking my head.

What the hell?

Once she opened the door, I quickly looked away and moved as far from her as I could.

"Hi, honey," Mom greeted, smiling at her.

"Hi, Aunt Bailey and Uncle Aiden," she replied in the sweetest voice with a nice big smile.

I rolled my eyes, wanting to throw up in my mouth.

She was not sweet or nice. She was the opposite of that, and I had her battle scars on my body to prove it.

Harley sat as close to me as possible, knowing it would annoy me, and I couldn't say anything about it in front of my parents.

She knew it too.

She was doing it on purpose.

I hate her.

I knocked her arm with my elbow, and she knocked mine back harder.

"Loser," she mouthed.

Grabbing my notebook from the seat pocket in front of me with her letters, I started a new one before throwing the whole pad of paper in her lap.

They r not your aunt or uncle. We r not your real family. We r way better than u. Y do u smell like the poop spray my mom sprays in the bathroom? U smell like a fruity fart.
–With all my hate for u, Jackson

She smiled, pulling out her stupid girly pen with the pink fluff on the end from her purse. I'd broken a few, but she always had more.

They ain't your parent's either cuz u were adopted. Did u not shower? I can smell your nuts from here.
–Not love, Harley

At least my parents wanted me. U were an accident turned into a big, huge mistake. U must be smelling yourself, ass face.
–With all my hate for u, Jackson

I'm so done with u.

–Not love, Harley

I'm always done with u. Blow me.
–With all my hate for u, Jackson

I'll blow u over.
–Not love, Harley

"What's going on back there?" Mom asked.

"Nothing," we replied at the same time.

Stop breathing my air.
-Not love, Harley

Ok, I'll strangle u, so u can't breathe at all.
-With all my hate for u, Jackson

Y don't u go play in trafic?
-Not love, Harley

Y don't u learn how to spell <u>traffic</u>?
-With all my hate for u, Jackson

She punched my leg where my parents couldn't see, and I tore the notebook from her lap.

U hit like a girl. Don't hit me again.
-With all my hate for u, Jackson

If I hit like a girl, then y u being a big baby about it? Build a bridge and get over it. Besides u started it.
-Not love, Harley

I didn't hit u, Gremlin.
-With all my hate for u, Jackson

Yeh, well u thought about it, Rudolph.
-Not love, Harley

I looked over at her and made a slicing gesture with my finger across my throat. Meaning it for her.

She grinned, squinting her eyes at me before snatching the notebook from my lap. Swiping right to my apology letters, like she knew they'd be there or something.

"Oh my God, Jackson! This is so mean and hurtful! Why would you give me this?" she exaggerated out loud, faking the offended tone in her voice. **"Dear Harley Gremlin Jameson,"** she started reading the first letter, the worst one my mom crossed out, for them to hear.

"My mom is making me write this apology letter to u. Like I would ever say sorry to the stupidest girl ever born. I don't surrender to Gremlins, I eat them for breakfast. You r so ugly the ambulance should take u away, so u can't get me in trouble anymore. I didn't do anything but tell u the truth. I CAN jump higher than u off the swings. It's not my fault u r just a stupid girl with no nuts, but even if u had nuts, they would be the size of raisins all shriveled up in your ugly face. Stop getting me in trouble or else I'm going to tell all my football friends u have a disease that's going to make their balls fall off and no one will talk to u when u get to middle school.

I hate u.

U suck for life.

With all my hate for u, Jackson

The demon even made her eyes water as she wiped away her fake tears. There were none.

I should have seen it coming, but I blamed her horrible outfit blinding me. Based on the huge disappointment spread across my parents faces while they shook their heads at me...

I was grounded.

Again.

Making me hate her even more.

But this wasn't the end. No, it was only the beginning.

It was now my turn...

To make her pay.

Chapter Five

Harley

"You have gotta be kiddin' me?" I gasped, lookin' at the stupid white tee my momma was holdin' up that read in bright red letters, "Our Get-Along Shirt".

"I'm not wearing that," Jackson agreed, starin' at it in horror the same way I was.

I thought my fakin' in the SUV would've saved me from havin' to be near him for the rest of the day at the clubhouse barbeque. Like his momma would've taken him home, not punish me by makin' us wear this huge shirt together.

"It don't even match my outfit," I stated, shakin' my head as fast as I could.

Jackson rolled his eyes, snappin', "The Halloween costume you're wearin' don't even match as an outfit."

I stepped on his foot cuz he was copying my accent. "Imma fashionista!"

"Ow!"

"That's what you get for makin' fun of my southern twang, bully Pierce!"

"You just stepped on my foot, and I'm the bully?"

"Yeah! And I'll do it again!"

"Enough!" Momma yelled out, makin' us look back at her. Disruptin' our hateful stares for each other. "Since you kids can't write a nice simple letter to each other, Bailey and I thought this would be the next best tactic."

"By punishing us some more? You already took away all my video games for the next month. Aren't I suffering enough? Now you're going to make me be stuck to her for the rest of the day? It's only noon, Mom! I'll die before the day is over."

"If only I could be so lucky," I sang, lookin' at him.

"Do you see what I have to deal with?" He pointed at me. "What do you think is going to happen if we're stuck together all day? I'll end up killing her, that's what."

"Not when I kill you first, you douchebag!"

"I said enough!" Momma shouted again. "You can both work it out *together*. The whole family is over this thing the two of you have taken too far. You need to learn to get along, even if it kills you."

"But, Momma—"

She shot me a warnin' stare before throwin' the shirt over both of our heads. Makin' the sides of our bodies touch.

"Ugh…" I tried to move away but the shirt choked me. I had no choice but to stay glued to him. "He's already makin' me hot."

"Ugh…" he repeated in the same voice I just used. "I'm already catching her stupid." He head-butted me. "Scoot over!"

"I can't cuz your big ass body is takin' up all the room!" I shoved him.

"Harley Jameson!"

"It is! I ain't got no room! You scoot over!" I shoved him again.

"Just let them work it out alone," Aunt Bailey stated, grabbin' my momma's arm.

She nodded.

"Alone?" Jackson hollered.

"*Yes*, alone," his mom answered, only lookin' at him. "You aren't allowed to be around anyone except each other today. All the other kids have been instructed to stay inside. You two are staying outside."

"So, you're going to make me sweat my nuts off too?"

"It's not that hot out, Jackson."

"*But, Momma*… Cash and Shiloh are already waitin' for me! We have church today to talk 'bout the moron standin' next to me."

"You're so obsessed with me."

"Ugh! Get over yourself. I'm not a stupid cheerleader."

"*Jealous*, Harley?"

"Of the twat waffles who don't got a brain cuz they like you? *Puh lease*…"

"Mom! I can already feel myself getting stupider just cuz she's

34

touching me."

"That's what she said, buttface! And you're touchin' me. I ain't touchin' you!"

They both just shook their heads in disappointment like always. That was the first time I realized everyone was inside and not runnin' around the compound.

I couldn't even find my daddy, which meant Momma musta' pulled her superpower rank. Where Daddy couldn't save me, or he'd get in big trouble too.

My eyes went to the window at the side of the clubhouse, and there was Shiloh and Cash watchin' us. Lookin' like I felt. Shiloh made a heart with her fingers for me, and I made one back for her. Except it was only half a heart cuz my other hand was inside the shirt, touchin' the boy I hated the most.

Ugh! They are ruinin' my life!

"Have fun and please try to work out your issues," Aunt Bailey ordered before they both turned and left us there.

Once Momma was at the front door of the clubhouse, she shouted, "And don't even think about taking that shirt off! We're watching you on the cameras!"

As soon as they were out of sight, Jackson burped really loud and blew it in my face. The smell of pickles and onions went up my nose, makin' me wanna puke.

I blew it back in his Rudolph face, but it didn't have the same effect as it did on me.

"You are absolutely disgustin'! What did you eat for breakfast? Your own butthole?"

He smiled, big and wide. The kind of smile that made me wanna knock his teeth out.

"No, it smells like I ate yours."

"I would never let you near my butthole."

"If I wanted near your butthole, then guess what, Gremlin… I'd be in there."

"In your dreams."

"No, it's actually in yours."

"Oh, trust me, Rudolph… when I see your face in my dreams, it's always a nightmare."

"Oh, so you *are* dreaming about me?" he asked with a cocky smirk on his face.

"No, stupid. They're nightmares like your breath. Now scoot

35

over!" I turned to face him and pushed him as hard as I could.

He tripped a little, takin' me with him.

"You jerk! You almost made me fall on you!"

"You pushed me!"

"Yeah! Well, you usually never move! So I must be gettin' strong enough to kick your ass!"

"You wish! I could take you down with one finger."

"Try it and watch how fast I break it off!"

"Oh my God! You're going to make me deaf with your loud ass mouth that never shuts up!"

"You never shut up! It's why I'm always in trouble, cuz of you and your big mouth!"

Out of nowhere he turned around and started walkin' fast…

Draggin' me with him.

Jackson

"You're walkin' too fast, butthole eater! I'm gonna fall!"

"So fall! Like I care!" I replied, annoyed and frustrated I was stuck to her whiny ass.

"If I fall, then you're comin' wit' me!"

Before I could respond, she threw her arms around my stomach. The entire front of her body stuck against the back of mine.

"Get off me, you spider monkey!"

"No! Slow down or we're gonna fall!"

I didn't stop, I was too pissed. Instead, I started jogging.

"Jackson, slow down!"

"Never!"

I ran faster, and for the most part, she kept up. Holding onto me tighter and tighter with each step.

"I can't breathe!"

"Good!"

"Harley! Let go!"

"Never!"

And then the little shit jumped on me, wrapping her legs around my waist with her free arm around my neck, choking me. It wasn't that I couldn't hold up her weight, I was used to dragging guys on me in football and she weighed nothing compared to them. It was the fact it had just rained that morning and the grass and dirt was still slippery.

My feet slid out from underneath me and the next thing I knew, I fell face first into the mud. Taking her with me.

Seconds later, I heard her laughing her butt off.

"Oh man!" She laughed harder. "That was so much better than I thought it was gonna be!"

When I lifted my head up from the nasty muck, she grabbed it and shoved me back down.

"That's for my Ken doll, murderin' his wife! He's never been the same!"

I jerked my head back, holding it up with all my strength, knowing she would do it again if given the chance. I warned, "You better run and hide, Harley!"

"I ain't scared of you!"

And with that, she grabbed a fistful of mud and slapped it into my face. Laughing again.

"Oh, it's on!"

"Bring it, dipwad!"

Before the last word left her mouth, I sat up and rolled us over, so I was now on top of her. The shirt stretched as far as it could, giving me more room to show her who was boss.

She gasped, "Jackson Pierce! Don't you dare—"

I smacked two handfuls of mud onto her face. "What was that, Harley Jameson? I can't hear you?"

"Jack—"

"I own you! Don't you ever forget that!" I smashed two more fistfuls onto her face. "What were you saying about kicking my ass? With what nuts, baby girl?"

In one quick movement, she pushed away, far enough to knee me in mine.

"Wit' *your* nuts, fart face!"

I rolled onto my back, groaning in pain.

You think that stopped her? Nope.

"I own you!" she repeated, smacking me with a pile of mud on my face, one right after the other. "And don't *you* ever forget it!"

"Harley Josie Jameson!" her mom screamed, making us both jump and knock heads. "Not even ten minutes! You couldn't even make it ten

37

minutes!"

"Uh oh," she whispered, and I used her shock of being caught to knock her over with a huge fistful of mud to the side of her face.

"Jackson Ashlyn Pierce!" my mom added, the two of them rushing toward us.

"I win. Always. Get up. Now. They're using our full names, so we're really in trouble."

Harley glared at me like she wanted to kill me, and I had the same expression on my face toward her.

"I. Hate. You."

"Not. As. Much. As. I. Hate. You," I reminded, meaning every last word.

We stood up at the same time, banging into each other. Wanting to be the first one standing.

"Stop," I clenched out, elbowing her.

"You stop." She elbowed me back.

"You both stop right now!" Mom ordered, and we did. We were standing side by side with our heads bowed. Covered head to toe in mud.

"What do you have to say for yourself, young lady?" her mom asked, now standing in front of us.

Harley shrugged, not looking up. "At least we didn't take the shirt off."

I nodded. She was right. I don't know how it was still on us, but it was. Hanging by a thread.

"Jackson, go get cleaned up," Mom demanded in the tone that meant I was screwed. "You have five minutes to get in the car, and we're going home. You have sufficiently ruined everyone's day."

"Sorry," I grumbled.

"No, you're not sorry. That's the worst part."

"I'm sorry for ruining your day, not for *her*."

"Enough. You say one more word and your father will be getting involved. Do you understand me?"

"Yes, ma'am."

I stepped out of the shirt and did as I was told. Not waiting another second, or who knew how much more trouble I'd be in, and I wasn't willing to find out.

Before Harley could say anything else out of her loud, stupid mouth, I left. Making my way over to the side of the clubhouse, out of sight.

I grabbed the hose and started washing myself off when I heard,

38

"Got your ass handed to ya by a girl. How's that feel, football star?"

My eyes snapped to Cash. My anger grew as soon as I heard his voice. Harley, I could handle. Cash was another story. We hated each other, but in a much different way than her and I.

Something about him pissed me off. I didn't know what it was, but it was there every time I saw him and Harley together. Which was a lot. They were attached at the hip.

The way they were together...

The way he defended her...

The way he played his guitar and sang her his stupid songs while she danced around...

The way...

The way...

The way...

Everything about their friendship was annoying. He thought he was better than me because his best friend was a girl. Harley wasn't even a pretty girl. She looked like a piñata exploded half the time. I had older girls who wanted me—*cheerleaders*.

All he had was Harley.

I smiled. "Not any different than her having you wrapped around her little finger, boy toy. Why don't you go running back to Harley, Cash? You can clean all the mud off her since she owns your nuts."

"Says the guy whose nuts she just kicked."

"Cash!" Shiloh hollered, bringing our attention over to her. "His mom is coming this way! You're going to get in trouble!"

"Better listen, Cash, or else they'll take away your guitar again, and then how will you bore everyone with your no talent?"

"I guess the same way you do at your football games."

"I'm the MVP, dickwad. Without me, they can't even play."

"Keep tellin' yourself that, Jackson. Since football is the only thing you got goin' for ya."

"Cash! Come on! You can fight with Jackson later! If you get grounded too, who am I going to hang out with?"

I laughed, "Go be with your other loser friend."

"At least I got a girl. *Two*, actually."

"Cash! I mean it! Bring your hide!"

He backed away, leaving me there.

God, I hate him.

The entire ride home was quiet, other than my mom saying I needed to head straight to the shower and then meet her in the kitchen after.

I did exactly that, hoping maybe my dad wouldn't be waiting with her when I came back down.

He was.

Crap.

Dad ordered, "Sit down, Son."

I nodded, taking a seat across from them at the island.

"Your mom is very upset with you, Jackson. I can't say I'm happy with you either. Especially since you know your mom has been stressed and overwhelmed this last year."

He was right. I did know that.

My mom was always the best mom she could be, but over the last year, she'd started forgetting things. Like picking us up from school or picking me up from football practice. She'd forget games, doctor appointments, even small things like her purse or car keys.

It wasn't like her at all, and I think it was because she took on too much. She never told any of us no, not even my dad. We were her whole entire world, and she never said this out loud, but I knew I was her favorite. I spent the most time with her, watching her stupid chick flicks, cooking with her. Anything she wanted to do, I was down for.

She was my mom, and I loved spending time with her. We had a special bond.

But nothing could have prepared me for what happened next…

Nothing.

Mom took one look at me and opened her mouth to say my full name, at least that's what I assumed, because every conversation when I was about to get grounded started that way. But nothing came out.

"Mom… are you okay?"

She just stared at me, almost like she couldn't get her mouth to say what she wanted. It didn't make any sense. She knew my name. She was my mom.

She named me.

"Mom…"

My eyes flew back to my dad, and for the first time in my life, I saw a look in his eyes I would never forget…

Fear.

And I just knew…

Our lives would never be the same again.

Chapter Six

Harley

Then: Nine years old

"So whatcha want to do this weekend?" Shiloh asked me, walkin' to our last class of the day. "Maybe we can go watch Cash's band rehearse?"

Cash started a band about six months before with some kids from our school. They practiced in each other's garages and were gettin' really good. Cash was the lead singer and guitarist, which drove the girls at our elementary school wild. It was nice to see Jackson's face anytime a ditzy cheerleader paid attention to Cash instead of him.

I made sure to rub it in his stupid, smug ego anytime I saw it going down in the hallways and believe me, it happened often. Jackson may have been the most popular boy at our school cuz he was starting quarterback for our city's little league, but that didn't change the fact girls liked Cash just as much.

"Oh, that'd be fu—" Out of nowhere, someone bumped into me from behind, sendin' all my notebooks flyin' out of my hands.

I didn't have to wonder who it was. I already knew.

"Walk much, loser?" Jackson mocked, standin' in front of us wearin' his stupid football jersey. His jock friend Trigger Reed in his jersey too next to him, both with huge grins spread across their stupid faces.

Trigger was the star defensive end, and the second most important player on the little league team. Together, they were the dynamic duo, and cuz of them, we were undefeated.

Barf.

They were best friends, who thought they were gods. The whole football team did. It was actually really irritatin', especially durin' the games. They'd walk through the field, chantin' and cheerin' as the crowd went wild. All the cheerleaders tryin' to get noticed as they strutted by.

Barf again.

It still blew my mind how girls swarmed to them like bees to honey.

In my eyes, they were all big fat douchebags with their brains in their biceps.

I didn't hesitate, steppin' toward him, but Shiloh grabbed my arm to hold me back.

"Hi, Principal Salisbury," she said, surprisin' me and savin' my butt for at least the hundredth time.

This wasn't over.

I was still pissed at Jackson for last night's prank. I don't know how or when he got in my room, but he put flour in my pillowcase at some point durin' the day.

After I went to bed, fresh out of the shower, I laid my wet head down and white powder exploded everywhere. I spent the next hour tryin' to get it out of my hair and sheets without my parents noticin'.

One of the things that changed between us in the last three years, we stopped tellin' on each other, cuz it always backfired. No matter who started it, we'd both get in trouble and be grounded.

Though, those weren't the only things that suddenly changed. Jackson's family started to come around less and less. I couldn't remember the last time I'd seen his parents at a Sunday barbeque. No one had any answers when I asked where they were. Sometimes my Uncle Noah and Aunt Skyler would bring the boys with them, but most of the time, they stopped comin' too.

Ever since our mud fight, somethin' shifted in Jackson's behavior toward me.

He was meaner…

Crueler…

An all-out bully to the max.

If that was even possible.

It was like overnight his hatred for me quadrupled, changing from pickin' on me to prankin' me endlessly in the evilest of ways.

And I wasn't just gonna stand back and take it.

Ever.

I always evened the score. No matter what, I paid him back.

Always.

"Kids, the second bell has rung. You're going to be late for class," Principal Salisbury announced, bringin' our stares over to him.

"We were just on our way, Sir. But, you see, Trigger and I just stopped to help Harley with her books," Jackson lied, smilin' at me. "Right, Harley?"

"Somethin' like that," I replied, smilin' back. Wantin' to punch his teeth out.

"That's very nice of you. Way to set an example for the other students," Principal Salisbury went on.

"Of course, Sir. We're always setting the bar high for the rest of the school. Lead by example is what our team stands for," Jackson added, and I think I threw up in my mouth a little.

How do people not see through his crap? Especially, girls.

He quickly bent down and grabbed all my books, handin' them back to me with an expression that screamed, '*I'm better than you.*' Archin' an eyebrow, he taunted, "Maybe try to work on not being so clumsy, Jameson. These textbooks cost our school a lot of money, and I'd hate for you to get into trouble for destroying school property."

O-M-G, I'm gonna kill him.

Shiloh intervened, readin' my mind. She grabbed my notebooks from his hands.

"Thanks for looking out, Jackson."

"Always here to help, Shiloh."

Jackson's butt buddy didn't waste any time, smilin' and noddin' over to Shiloh in that *Trigger Reed* sort of way. The one that made girls blush, swoon, and melt all at once.

Bigger barf.

"Maybe we'll see you around this weekend," he flirted, winkin' at her.

Ummm… no, we hate you.

"Probably not," she bit, makin' me smile at him. I held back on givin' him the stank face cuz it would only get me in trouble.

Trigger bumped into Jackson's arm in some bro code kind of way, and I gripped onto Shiloh's elbow and rushed us into our classroom before I said somethin' I regretted.

I was about to take my seat next to her desk, but Jackson tripped

43

me. *Again.* Almost knockin' my books out of my hands. *Again.*

From behind me, he whispered into my ear, "What did I tell you about watching where you're going, baby girl?" He was standin' too close to my back, and I could feel his hatred for me pourin' out of him. It was stingin' a hole into my body.

On reflex, I elbowed him in his ribs, but he blocked it and slapped my butt.

"Bad girl."

"You fresh pig—"

"Hush up, Harley." He tugged me closer to his chest with his fingers gripping my hip. His lips were now brushin' against my ear. "The teacher is watching. Don't get us in trouble cuz you can't control that short Jameson fuse."

My mouth dropped open.

"Are you going to cry?"

"Never."

"Maybe next time."

"Keep dreamin', turd munch."

I turned to look at him, but he moved away and went to his desk in the back of the classroom.

Nothin' was worse than endin' my Friday to his Rudolph face.

Since this class was an elective, it was a mixture of all grades. My choices were either Language Arts or P.E., and I didn't want to sweat.

However, I loved to read. It was one of my favorite things to do. Shiloh, Cash, and I always chose our classes together, but he dipped out on this one. I wasn't surprised to see Jackson in here, though. He was probably doing it to pick up chicks.

Ignorin' his dumbass face I could still feel starin' at me, I sat down at my desk and brushed him off. Thinkin' about Trigger instead.

Rippin' out a sheet of paper from my notebook, I started writin'.

What crawled up Trigger's butt and died?

As soon as Mr. Lenyard turned his back to start class and wrote somethin' on the board, I threw my note on Shiloh's desk.

Probably the nearest cheerleader.

U think he likes u?

44

Eww… gross. I hope not. Like I would ever fall for a boy like him. He's a football player. I hate football. And he uses girls. I heard he's already gone to 2nd base.

Whose boobs did he touch?

More like whose hasn't he touched…

I wonder if Jackson has gone to 2nd base?

You're thinking about Jackson and boobs?

Why was I thinkin' about him and boobs?
"Yes, Jackson?" Mr. Lenyard called out, makin' me look up.
"I'm trying to pay attention, but Harley's passing notes and it's really distracting."
So much for not tellin' on each other.
"Harley, if what you're talking about is so important, why don't you share it with the class?" Jackson baited, knowin' it would embarrass me.
"No thanks," I responded. "I'm good." Hopin' Mr. Lenyard wouldn't make me.
"Actually, I think that's a great suggestion, Jackson. How about you share what's so important it couldn't wait until after class, Miss Jameson?"
"I don't think that's—"
"I can't hear you all the way back here, Harley. I think you should stand up and talk louder for those of us in the back," Jackson continued on, and I never wanted to slap the stupid out of him more than I did in that second.
I glared at him. "I don't think—"
"Another great suggestion, Jackson. Please stand, Miss Jameson."
I grumbled under my breath.
"What was that, Harley?" he baited again.
"I said, *sure*… that sounds like a great idea."
"Well, don't keep us all waiting."
"That's enough, Mr. Pierce."
I swallowed hard, bitin' my bottom lip before slowly standin'.
What do I make up? Maybe I'll say—
The class immediately started laughin' and pointin' at me, except

for Shiloh. Whose eyes were wide as saucers.

I looked around the room. "What's goin—"

Shiloh jumped into action, takin' off her sweater and rushin' over to me. Wrappin' it around my waist.

"What?" I coaxed, lookin' at her. Not understandin' what was goin' on.

When Greg announced, "Looks like Aunt Flo came for a visit, Harley," the class laughed louder and harder.

My eyes shot to Jackson. He was leanin' back in his chair with his arms crossed over his chest. A huge smile spread across his face with a gleam in his eyes.

He shrugged. "I guess that's why you've been so bitchy."

The class fell into a fit of laughter, and Mr. Lenyard shouted, "Mr. Pierce!" Then he warned, "Class that's enough!"

Shiloh could see it in my eyes, they were gettin' watery.

"Hold it in, babe. Not here. Not now."

I nodded, bitin' my bottom lip again.

It was then that she pulled the squished ketchup packets from my back pockets, and I screamed out, "Jackson! You set me up!"

He put his hand on his chest, fakin' bein' hurt. "I wish I could see what you're talking about, but I can't get my head that far up your butt."

My eyes widened. "Look!" I yelled at him, showin' everyone the splattered packets in my hands. "You put these in my back pockets, so it'd look like my friend came! When it didn't, you lyin' piece of poo!"

"Am I supposed to be offended? Because the only thing offending me is your face."

Mr. Lenyard snapped, "That's enough, you two!"

"Drop it, Harley. You're going to get detention. Don't let him ruin your weekend too," Shiloh muttered, tryin' to calm me down.

She was right.

The last thing I wanted to do was let Jackson think he won, but it was the only choice I had. I went and cleaned up in the bathroom as best as I could. Sitting back down in my chair, where I ignored him for the rest of class.

Plottin' my revenge.

Chapter Seven

Harley

As soon as Shiloh and I saw my memaw pull into the car line at school, we rushed toward her SUV. Prayin' no one would see me.

At least not anyone else.

"Honey, what's wrong?" Memaw Alex asked as I jumped into the front seat and Shiloh got into the back.

"Go! Go! Go!" I shouted, before closing the door behind me.

I needed to get out of there, and it needed to happen fast.

She didn't wait, steppin' on the gas and doing exactly that. Out of every adult in my life, she was the one who understood me the most. She said I reminded her a lot of her best friend Lily, who was Shiloh's Momma and my papaw's baby sister, with a mix of my momma.

It was an ongoin' joke between them. Shiloh acted more like my grandma Alex. She was "The Mom" of the good ol' kids like Memaw had been to the good ol' boys.

Shiloh was the responsible one.

Super mature, always had been.

She'd never fall for a boy like Trigger. He was definitely barkin' up the wrong tree with her.

"Let me guess," Memaw stated, bringin' my thoughts back to the boy I hated the most. "Jackson Pierce."

"UGH! You won't believe what he did to me! I'm gonna kill him. Like I'm really gonna murder him! I'm gonna go to jail!" I looked over at her. "Will you bail me out?"

She tried to hide back a laugh.

You see, Memaw Alex wasn't a regular grandma… she was a cool one.

I still remembered the day a few years ago when she bought me a couple pairs of heart sunglasses at the Fourth of July parade in Southport. She never confirmed it, but I suspected she bought me those for one reason and one reason only.

To block out Jackson.

"You look stupider than you normally do, wearing those sunglasses," Jackson harassed when he saw me wearin' them for the first time.

I lifted my head higher, not payin' him any mind. Pretendin' as if he wasn't there.

"Hello!" he shouted near my face. "Did you hear me? Or have I finally gotten my wish and your loud ass mouth can't talk anymore?"

Still, nothin'. I couldn't see him.

"She can't hear you, dummy. She's wearing her Jackson Blockers," Shiloh answered for me.

"Her what?" he replied, confused.

"Her Jackson Blockers. You're invisible when she has them on, duh!"

He didn't wait for one second, steppin' in front of my face and rippin' them off. Immediately throwin' them on the floor, he stepped on them. Crushin' them into millions of pieces.

I just stood there not carin'. "It don't matter. I have back-ups."

"Yeah?" He cocked his head to the side with a nasty look in his eyes. Starin' only at me. "I'll break those too."

"Memaw! This is not a laughin' matter! He took it too far this time! O-M-G!" I laid my head back on the headrest. "I hate him so freakin' much!"

"Calm down. What happened?"

I sat up, pullin' Shiloh's sweater away to show her the back of my jeans. "This happened!"

"You got your peri—"

"NO! Jackson put ketchup packets in my back pockets, and I didn't even notice! And now the whole classroom thinks I got my period today!"

Shiloh chimed in, "Harley, they don't think that. You showed them the proof. Everyone knows Jackson and you have this ongoing prank war."

"It don't matter! I can't ever go back to school! I'm gonna have to move to another state! You think I could go under witness protection?"

"Harley, take a deep breath," Memaw ordered in a soft tone, and I did as I was told.

"Take another one... that's it... in and out..."

I felt a little better, but not much.

"Everyone is gonna be talkin' 'bout it at school on Monday. I can never show my face in public again."

"I know it feels that way now, honey, but it won't feel that way tomorrow. I promise."

"You swear?"

"Would I ever lie to you?"

I shook my head no.

"I think it's time I let you both in on a little secret. You're old enough to hear it now."

"What?" we replied at the same time.

"Now, I know this is going to sound like the craziest thing I have ever said, but I promise you what I'm about to tell you is nothing but the truth."

"Okay..."

I waited on pins and needles for what she was about to share, never expectin' her to say, "Jackson is mean to you because he likes you."

I looked at her like she was crazy. "Wait, what?"

"I know. Sounds insane, right? I get it. But that's just how boys are. They bully, tease, taunt, just because they don't know what else they can do to get your attention. And nothing gets your attention more than hurting your feelings."

"Memaw, that don't make any sense."

"I know, sweet girl, but boys don't make any sense. It's best that you realize that now. Because they don't get any better as they get older."

"Uncle Lucas picked on you?" Shiloh asked, readin' my mind.

"Honey, Lucas still picks on me. He just does it in other ways."

"Like when he won't let you win at Monopoly and buys all the best real estate?" I asked next, eyein' Shiloh who looked just as confused as I was.

"Girls, I'm going to let you in on another little secret."

"There's more?"

"So much more."

"Is there like a club we can join? Or a book on this?"

"No, honey... no club or book. Just worldly knowledge that comes

49

with age."

"Well, how old do we gotta be?"

"A lot older."

I sighed. "All the good stuff happens when we're a lot older, like drivin' motorcycles. And we been knowin' how to drive those since we were six cuz of the MC."

Shiloh smiled. It was true, we could drive motorcycles as good as any boy ever could. Better even.

"So, what's the big secret?" Shiloh questioned.

"Well… I *let* Lucas beat me at Monopoly."

"Memaw! Why would you ever let him beat you? Losin' is the worst feelin' ever!"

"Because, Harley Jameson, it makes him feel good, and sometimes you just gotta let them feel like an alpha."

"But they ain't dogs."

"Debatable."

"So, let me get this straight. You're fixin' to tell us that for the last bazillion years you guys have been together, you, Alex Ryder—mother of my momma, who never lets Daddy win at anythin' if she can help it—that you lose on purpose?"

"Yep, that's what I'm telling you."

"Memaw, that's the dumbest thing I ever heard. I don't lose. I'm a Jameson. *We* don't lose. *Ever.* Especially to that turd, *Jackson Pierce.*"

"One day, baby, trust me… you won't feel that way."

"Why? Cuz girls get dumber as they get older?"

"Yes. Especially when it comes to love."

"But I hate Jackson Pierce. I even use my birthday wishes on him. Do you understand how serious that is? I get one birthday a year, one wish a year, and I use it on him. And you know what I wish?"

"What, baby? What do you wish?"

"For him to *lose* and for me to *win*, at everythin' and anythin'. That's not too much to ask, right? You would think it wouldn't be, but the wish fairy ain't listenin' to me cuz sometimes I lose. Like today! Epic, epic loss!"

"Harley, maybe she's right."

"Shiloh, bite your tongue. I would never let him win—"

"No, not about that. About Jackson liking you. It kinda makes sense. He follows you around just waiting for you to react to him."

"He does it to torture me."

"Yeah, because you pay attention to him. I mean, how many

50

Jackson Blockers has he broken since you started wearing them? He breaks them the second he sees them on you. Why? Because he doesn't want you to ignore him."

"Right, so he can keep torturin' me."

"No. So you can keep paying attention to him. I think Aunt Alex is onto something. Jackson likes you."

Little did I know the next words that came out of Shiloh's mouth would haunt me for the rest of my life.

When she added, "And maybe… he even loves you."

Chapter Eight

Jackson

Then: Ten years old

Nineteen…
Twenty…
Twenty-one…
Twenty-two…
Twenty-three…

"Hey, Mom," I greeted, walking into her room.

It always took twenty-three steps.

Twenty-three seconds.

Twenty-three pounding heartbeats to get to see her again.

She looked up from whatever she was lost in and smiled at me. "Hi," she breathed out with glossy, drained eyes.

She always looked so tired, like she was constantly battling something within herself.

An all-out war for her sanity and peace of mind.

Turning away from her, I sat my backpack and the sunflowers I picked on the way over on the chair. Holding my head down for a few moments to catch some air.

Breathe in and out, Jackson.

In and out.

Just. Keep. Breathing.

I needed a second to get my shit together. I always did. It didn't matter how many times I told myself this was going to get easier. It never did. If anything, it always got harder.

Nothing about the woman in front of me reminded me of my mother.

Her eyes.

Her smile.

Her laugh

Not even...

Her love.

"Don't you have school?" she asked out of nowhere, making my eyes snap back to hers.

I smiled. I couldn't help it. There was no hiding the relief I felt.

"I did. I came here right from school. It's Friday. Your favorite day."

She mirrored my expression, stating, "Because all my boys are home for two whole days."

My eyes watered, there was no hiding that either. Feeling an overwhelming amount of emotion because she was having a good day.

I never knew what was worse... when she remembered or when she didn't.

Me. Her. Us.

She still had more good days than bad. However, when they were bad, they were the worst.

"Yeah, Mom. Two whole days with all your boys home."

"I cooked your favorite dinner. Pot roast with no carrots."

I chuckled, "I hate carrots. They're such a pointless vegetable. They taste like nothing."

"But they're so good for your mind. You need to be like your daddy, not like me. Never like me."

"Mom, do you want me to brush your hair?" I asked, changing the subject.

"Oh, yes! I'd love that," she replied, her eyes sparkling.

I hated when she looked at me like that. As if she was trying to make a memory of my face, of this moment, of this day.

Of *me*.

She shouldn't have to. She should just know.

But she didn't.

Nothing about this was fair. Not when it all started, not when we found out what was happening, not anything that followed.

My feet moved on their own accord. Inch by inch, step by step, I made my way over to her with the sunflowers and brush in my hand.

Her eyes widened, beaming. "My favorite."

I nodded. "Yeah, Mom. Sunflowers are your favorite." My chest tightened with each second that passed between us.

Little by little, it felt as if I was losing more and more air the closer I got to her. My heart was in my throat, beating a mile a minute.

Breathe, Jackson. Don't stop breathing.

Closing my eyes, I swallowed hard before I was standing in front of her.

"Are you okay?"

"Yeah," I lied. "I'm fine."

"Why do you look so sad?"

I opened my eyes, staring right into hers. "Cuz I love you," I blurted without thinking.

"Honey, I love you too."

I shut my eyes again, fighting back the tears.

Stay strong. You need to stay strong.

Kids should never have to experience this. No one should ever have to experience something like this. They say when you go through trauma—a drastic, life-altering change—you're suddenly forced to grow up. Become wiser beyond your years. Mature in ways that didn't make sense except to the people who may have experienced similar events.

All of that was true, but every time I was with her, I felt like the boy, the kid, the child I was supposed to be.

Her son.

Her firstborn.

Her favorite.

I wanted my mom back. I wanted her more than anything.

I had a life three years ago. I had everything I could ever ask for. I lived in a home full of love and laughter. We were a perfect family. My parents had a perfect marriage.

All of it now a distant memory.

Thinking about the way things used to be made my heart ache. At times, it hurt so bad, I couldn't breathe. I had to remind myself to inhale and exhale.

In and out. In and out.

I woke up every night from nightmares and had no one to comfort me. No one to hold me and tell me everything was going to be all right.

No one to tell me they loved me.

That they would always love me.

My mother I'd known was gone, and I was left with nothing. With no one. The last thing I wanted was to cause her additional stress, knowing it wouldn't get me anywhere. It was one of her biggest triggers, only causing her to leave me faster.

That's what hurt the most.

Being alone with only my thoughts, my fears, the reality it could be me one day in her shoes. Laying in that bed, praying, hoping I would remember my life in the end.

I shook my head, trying to push what ate away at me every day.

My mind had become my own worst enemy.

Far greater than Harley Jameson could ever be.

"Jackson, come here, baby."

I didn't have to be told twice, and I went to her. Holding on for dear life.

Please... please don't leave me.

"Shhh... it's alright... I'm here..." she whispered, holding onto me just as tight. It was only then I realized I was crying.

"But for how long?"

"I don't know, baby. I just don't know anymore. I'm sorry, Jackson. I'm so sorry this is happening."

I leaned into her embrace, soaking it up as much as possible until I couldn't take it anymore, so I let it out.

I cried, harder and harder for I don't know how long. She didn't let go or push me away. If anything, she held me tighter, letting me sob for as long as I needed. Whispering reassuring words to help ease my pain and the hurt I felt all over.

"Please don't leave me, Mom. I won't make it without you. My heart hurts so much. Sometimes it hurts so bad that I feel like I'm dying, and it never ends. It's there. In my mind. Thinking about you... about our family... about what's going to happen when you're not here anymore... I think about it all. I don't want you to go. I don't want to lose you. I don't want to lose myself," I sobbed, unable to control my emotions and needing to tell her how I felt. "What is the point of living life if I may not remember it?"

I sucked in air, trying to find some sort of reassurance.

Waiting.

Feeling as though I was always waiting.

Her hold on me loosened, and I was suddenly filled with despair. Knowing what was coming. I shut my eyes tighter, holding onto her. Praying it would be enough to keep her there with me. That was the worst part of this, losing her over and over again.

"Mom… please… fight it… for me… please fight it for me…"

That one syllable.

Those three letters.

The first word I ever said.

The one she taught me, a word that was supposed to mean the world to her. Turned out to be her biggest trigger to leave me through it all.

But it wasn't until she spewed, "I'm not your mother," that she killed me once and for all.

"No! No! No! Don't do this! Don't do this to me! You're in there! I know you're still in there!"

"Get. Off. Me."

"Mom, plea—"

"I said, get off me!"

I shuddered at the sound of her voice, her tone laced with nothing but anger and hate. It was so easy for her to lose control. In seconds, she'd go from being my mother to a woman I didn't know. Who didn't know me.

"Fight for me!" I shouted, trying to get through to her. "I'm your son! Your Jackson! I'm all you ever wanted! Remember me! Please just remember me!"

"Get out!" she seethed from deep inside her, vibrating my entire body. Gripping onto the side of my arms, she tried throwing me off, but I didn't let go.

I couldn't.

I wouldn't.

Not when I'd just had her.

"I don't know you! I don't know you!"

"Yes, you do! You made me!"

"Get off!"

"Mom—"

"My name is Bailey! I'm not your mom! My name is Bailey! Get out! I said, get out!"

"NO!" I screamed with everything inside of me, my chest heaving, my heart breaking. "You're my mom! You're supposed to love me! Be there for me! That's your job!" I sobbed uncontrollably, hanging on by a thread.

"Dr. Pierce!" she called out for a man who wasn't even there. "Get him out! Get him out of here right now!"

"He's not your doctor! He's your husband! We're your family!" I heaved, struggling to breathe in and out. To hold on to whatever I had left of her.

"Jackson, you can't do this. It's not good for her," one of the nurses ordered, grabbing ahold of me. Prying me off her. "You have to go."

"Fuck you! She's my mother!"

"Not right now she's not. You're making matters worse!"

Tears flooded my eyes, spilling over and rolling down the sides of my face. "How can they get any worse than her not knowing who I am?!"

"I'm sorry, son, but you have to go."

My fingers held onto anything I could, snatching the heart necklace from my mom's neck. It was the only thing she had left from her childhood, belonging to her mother before she left her behind too.

"Don't take me away from her! Please don't take me away from her!"

I had no control over my emotions, not one.

"Keep him away from me! Keep him away from me!" she repeated in a tone that would forever haunt me. "I hate you! Do you understand me?! I. Hate. You!"

"Son, calm down!" I heard the nurse say over the ringing in my ears.

She hates me.

My mother hates me.

I stopped fighting, the wind knocked out of me. Every ounce of strength, of willpower, of love I had for her…

Was gone.

I watched her lose her mind.

Lose herself.

There was nothing left for me to do.

She was gone.

Again…

But for how long?

"I hate him! I never want to see him again! Don't let him come back! Please! Just keep him away from me!"

The look on her face.

The sound of her voice.

The way she was rejecting me.

It was all too much to take, too much to handle, too much to live through. Because in the back of my mind, all I could think, all I could see, all I could feel, was her not remembering me.

Out of everyone in her life…

She forgot me first.

And all I could think about was…

How much time, how many years, how much longer did I have…

Until I lost my mind too.

Chapter Nine

Harley

"Jackson doesn't look like he's in the best mood right now, Harley. Maybe it's not a good time to bring this up," Shiloh stated while we were at my daddy's Sunday MC barbeque.

Cash, Shiloh, and I were hangin' in the shed away from everyone else. I needed to be alone with my best friends at a time like this. We needed to talk about the atomic bomb that was dropped on me two days ago by Memaw when she picked us up from school.

I'd be lyin' if I said I wasn't surprised Jackson and Jagger were there in the first place. Especially after the stunt Jackson pulled in class. They'd come with Uncle Noah and Aunt Skyler, and it was the first time in what felt like months since they stepped foot on the compound.

Though Shiloh was right, Jackson looked like he'd seen better days. I'd spent the entire weekend thinkin' about what Memaw said. I couldn't help it. I wanted to rub it in Pierce's ugly face. I finally knew the truth behind his wicked ways.

He liked me.

Maybe even loved me.

"It's ridiculous you're even feedin' into that gibberish," Cash chimed in, pullin' my attention over to his eyes. "Is this why you're all gussied up? For him?"

"What?" I replied, taken back. "I ain't gussied up."

"You're as pretty as a peach today, Harley."

I smiled. "Really?"

"I knew it!"

I rolled my eyes, shakin' my head. "Cash, I always look good. It's just how I roll."

"You never wear makeup."

"I ain't wearin' makeup."

He stepped toward me and swiped his thumb over my lips, showin' me the pink residue left on his skin.

"That ain't lipstick. I ate a cherry popsicle earlier."

"Harley, you ain't foolin' anyone but yourself."

"I just wanna embarrass him like he embarrassed me."

"I think there's more to it than that."

"Like what?"

"I don't know, Harley. You tell me."

"I did tell you. What more do ya want me to say?"

"The truth."

"Which is?"

"I don't know, Harley. You tell me," he repeated in a much different tone.

"What's with the 'tude?"

"I don't like seein' you fussin' over a jackass. He ain't worth it."

"I ain't fussin' over him."

"He's all you've talked 'bout all weekend."

"That's only cuz he pissed me off."

"He always pisses you off, but you never talk 'bout him this much."

"Cash, my whole literature class thinks I got my period Friday. It's a little traumatizin', don't ya think?"

"Since when do ya care what people think 'bout you?"

"Since they think I was bleedin' out of my fruity tooty!"

Shiloh started laughin'.

"It ain't funny, girl."

"You're right. It wasn't funny then, but it's kinda funny now."

"Oh really? Was it funny when Trigger was sniffin' around your fruity tooty?"

"Ugh, gross. I can't stand him."

I looked over at Cash who was now strummin' on his guitar.

"Oh, I'm sorry," he said, catchin' my dumbfounded gaze. "I stopped listenin' when you started talkin' 'bout bleedin'."

Shiloh and I laughed.

Boys.

They can kill spiders, but the second you talk about girly things,

60

they're out like a trout.

"If you're worried I now love Jackson back or somethin', you're wrong. I don't even like him, Cash. You should know that more than anyone."

"Girls are weird." He shrugged. "Remember, I got three older sisters. Giselle is the weirdest of 'em all. How many years have her and your Uncle Mason been playin' games wit' each other?"

"Forever."

"See," he shrugged again. "Girls are weird."

"Boys are way weirder than girls, Cash."

"Facts," Shiloh agreed, noddin' with me.

"How do ya figure?"

"Cuz look at Jackson. Do you see this scar?" I pointed to my elbow. "I got this when he told me I couldn't climb the tallest tree right outside this shed. Turned out, I could. I just couldn't get down. Now these," I pointed to my knees, "I got them cuz he said I couldn't skateboard as fast as he could. Turned out, I totally can. I just don't know how to stop." I pointed to the scar on my hairline. "Now this one. You remember this one, right?"

"Yeah, we all got grounded for that one," Cash answered, shakin' his head. "I spent twenty minutes tryin' to talk you out of doin' it, and I still got in trouble."

I put my hands on my hips. "I landed it, didn't I?"

"Harley, you weren't supposed to land it. When you BMX off a ramp into a lake, the bike stays out in front of you."

"I know. I just forgot that part."

"It cost ya four stitches and a month of us all bein' grounded cuz that dickweed dared you."

"Exactly!"

He squinted his eyes at me, confused.

"You're provin' my point."

"How?"

"I have tons of scars from Jackson darin' me to do somethin'. They're all over my body, and every time I look at any of them, I remember how I got it in the first place. Don't ya see? Do ya get it now? Scars are permanent, Cash. They don't just go away."

"You're reachin', Harley."

"Naw uh."

"Come on, Cash, you gotta admit. It kinda makes sense," Shiloh chimed in. "He's been obsessed with Harley since we were babies. How many times has your mom told us the story about Jackson tripping Harley when she took her first step? They even have a picture of him laughing about it."

"More facts." I nodded.

"You're right about one thing."

"What's that?"

"Jackson does love you," Cash agreed. "He just *loves* to hate you."

"Maybe he thinks she's his lobster," Shiloh added, repeatin' what her mom always said about lobsters. A lobster was your soulmate, cuz they mate for life. The thought of Jackson thinkin' I was his lobster.

Well that…

I wasn't prepared for.

"Oh wow," I breathed out with wide eyes. "Jackson wants me to think about him forever cuz he wants me to be his lobster. Guys! Jackson is totally in love with me!"

Everythin' was good for about a second until that sentence came flyin' out of my mouth. I never wanted to eat my words as much as I did in that moment.

The person I least expected decided to walk right in and humiliate me even more.

Shoutin', "You think I love you, Gremlin?!"

Jackson

"You think I love you, Gremlin?!" I called her out, stalking into the shed.

Harley instantly turned when she heard my voice, not backing down.

"How long have you been listenin' to us?" she replied, locking eyes with me.

"Long enough to hear your fairytale story. So what, baby girl? I'm your Prince Charming now?"

"Don't call me that."

I never expected this turn in events when I walked over here to just be alone. I didn't even want to come today, but Noah made me. This was the last place I wanted to be.

Around so much happiness, so much laughter, so much love…
When my life was none of those things.

I wanted to shut down, to run away, to just stop thinking about tomorrow. It was like a ticking time bomb in my mind.

Tick…

Tick…

Tick…

Boom!

How much time did I have?

With my mom?

My dad?

My family?

My mind?

My memories?

My future?

Seconds, minutes, hours, days, months, years…

My life came down to nothing but time. Grieving the loss of a person who was still alive. Knowing it didn't end with her.

It had only just started.

Thinking solely of that, I zeroed in on Harley. Eyeing her up and down as I made my way over to her.

Rasping, "What if I do love you, Harley? What then?"

She jerked back, caught off guard by my question. Unexpectedly waiting for my next move. I'd beat her at her own game, I always did. But like anything with Harley, she would never surrender. It was what made fighting with her so amusing and addicting. She always stuck up for herself, no matter what.

Even if I embarrassed her.

Even if I tried to make her cry.

Even if I hurt her.

Even if…

Even if…

Even if…

She stayed strong.

She was a little shit like that.

But I was undeterred. I'd keep trying to make her fall apart, in hopes it would keep me together.

"You were talking up a storm before I walked in. Chatting a mile a minute, and now what? You got nothing to say? Easier to talk behind my back than to my face?" I arched an eyebrow at her, mocking her fruity tooty comment, *"Right, Toots?"*

"Whatever I say when you're not around, I'll say to your face," she sassed, stepping toward me. Exactly how I knew she would. "I know the truth now."

"Is that so?"

"Yes, that's so. I know you like me. The secret is outta the bag. Memaw explained it to Shiloh and me. You don't gotta hide it or pretend anymore."

"I don't?"

"Nope, but I'd *love* to tell ya, Jackson Pierce, that I, Harley Jameson, don't love you back. At all. Never. Ever. Ever. Ever, will I love you back."

I put my hand over my chest. "Way to crush a guy's heart, baby girl."

"I said don't call me that."

"What am I supposed to do now that you know the truth, Harley? You know I like you. I've always liked you." I leaned in close to her face. "But what if I even love you?"

"Jackson, stop messin' around," Cash interrupted, making my eyes snap to his.

"Mind your business, boy toy."

"Don't talk to him that way."

"Harley! Don't need ya to defend me against this tool. He's just playin' wit' ya."

"You jealous, Cash? That I got what you want?"

"What?" Harley blurted out. "Cash don't want me. We're just best friends."

"Keep telling yourself that. He's your little bitch for a reason."

"The only bitch I see in front of me is you, Pierce," he challenged, his hands fisting at his sides.

"What, Cash? You going to hit me?"

He shook his head no. "I don't gotta." Nodding to Harley, he added, "Cuz she will."

And she did just that. She shoved me, but I didn't budge.

"Back off! Cash is right, you are messin' with me."

"I'll just have to prove it to you then."

Shiloh coaxed, "Jackson, that's enough. You're getting everyone's feathers ruffled up over nothing."

"I thought Harley was my lobster? Isn't that what you said?"

"You weren't supposed to hear that."

"Isn't this what every girl wants? To be seen? To be heard? Noticed by me? Well, I'm standing right in front of you, Toots, telling you that I see you. You've got my attention now, Harley. What are you going to do with it?"

"I don't love you. I don't even like you. Especially right now. You're actin' weird."

"Guys are weird, right?" I parroted her earlier comment.

"Holy crap! How long were you listenin'? What game are you playin', Jackson?"

"The game we've always played. Get Harley to pay attention to me. I dare you to scar you. That's all I want. *You*, forever. I pick on you, I bully you, I tease you cuz I want you. Well, guess what, baby girl? You want me too."

"You're takin' this too far, dickweed! Stop!"

I didn't hesitate, jolting my stare to Cash. "Make me, pussy boy!"

He stepped forward, stopped by Shiloh's grip on his arm. "You said it earlier, Cash. He ain't worth it."

"I been wantin' to give him an ass whoopin' since preschool."

"I'm standing right here, boy toy. Let's see what ya got."

"Stop!" Harley ordered, putting her hands on my chest. "This is between you and me, so leave him out of it."

"Fine." I got right in her face, our noses almost touching. "I'll just show you how much I love you then."

Snapping, "Let me kiss you, Harley. That's what you want, right? Since I love you so much."

Chapter Ten

Jackson

"You can kiss my grits, Jackson."

"Baby girl, I just want to show you how much I've always loved you. I don't care if your friends see..."

She stepped back as I went forward four steps. Backing her into the wall, I caged her in with my arms.

She held her head up higher, not folding. Always too stubborn for her own damn good. I could see it in her eyes, no one knew Harley like I did.

Bottom line, I was getting to her.

Which was why I spoke the magic words, "*I dare you* to let me kiss you."

She jerked back, caught off guard again. Suddenly realizing she had nowhere to go.

All mine.

"The Harley I know and *love* never backs down from a dare." My eyes shifted to her lips, baiting, "I promise you'll like it."

Her stare landed on her friends, who were both about to blow a gasket in the corner. Watching us.

Especially Cash McGraw.

Two birds with one stone.

My lucky day.

"Come on, Harley. I. Dare. You."

She sucked in a breath before biting her bottom lip.

"You ready?" I taunted.

"No."

"Good. I like taking things from you anyway."

"You're the reason I can't have nice things."

I scoffed out a chuckle. "Shut up and close your eyes."

"Harley! You can't be serio—" Cash interjected.

"Screw off, McGraw!"

"Fine. I'll let you kiss me."

"What?!" Shiloh and Cash shouted simultaneously.

"But if you stick your tongue in my mouth, I'll bite it off."

"Harley! Don't let him steal your first kiss!" Shiloh shared.

I cocked my head to the side. "You've never been kissed?"

She blushed, shrugging. "So."

I already knew that, but it was still shocking to hear the words fall from her lips.

"I ain't like those brainless cheerleaders that will let anyone kiss them. Includin' you."

"Says the girl who just said I could kiss her."

"Only cuz you dared me. You know I can't turn down any of your dares. Even if they get me in trouble. I don't back down for anyone. I'm a Jameson. I'm a badass mothafucka. I ain't made that way."

I grinned. Her feisty personality always got to me. She was the perfect enemy, up for anything. The challenge of our dares, pranks, the ongoing war between us was as addicting to her as it was for me.

"So, I'll let you steal my first kiss."

"Harley! It's your first kiss! Don't do this!" Shiloh countered, further pissing me off. "It's too important to you. He just wants to hurt your heart. Don't let him take something that means so much away from you. He ain't worth it!"

Knowing this meant something to her.

That it was significant.

Cherished.

Guarded.

Only made me want to steal it even more.

Needing to show her who was boss.

Me.

Forever.

I owned her. She belonged to me, and she proved it every single time she said yes, because Harley never said no.

"Shiloh, why don't you learn how to shut your mouth?"

Harley pushed me. "Don't talk to her like that. She's just lookin' out for me, you kiss stealer!"

Cash's hands were still fisted at his sides, getting tighter and tighter the longer this went on. Only fueling my hatred for him. This was going to hurt him, and that fact alone made kissing Harley much more satisfying.

"Leave her alone!" he roared.

"Hey, tough guy! Which one? Harley or Shiloh?"

"I said leave her alone!"

"Oh, so it's Harley again? Why? Are you going to take her place? You want me to bully you? You never learn, do you, Cash?"

"What was that?"

"You heard me. Grow some balls already, bro. Unless you don't have any cuz you're really a girl . Always being Harley's protector, but news flash... I'll always be in her life too."

"That's funny comin' from you, Jackson. The only thing you want is attention. You're a jock who walks around school thinkin' you're untouchable. That every girl wants you and every guy wants to be ya. You treat everyone like shit and just expect them to fall at your feet. You can't stand the fact Harley doesn't want ya. So you have these pranks, these dares, all this bullshit just to get her attention. Newsflash, Jackson... *I* will always be in Harley's life when you have nothin'. No one other than your dumbass jock friends, who only like you cuz you're popular. I have somethin' you will never have and you can't stand it. Who has the bigger balls now, bro?"

"I'll show all y'all who has bigger balls..." Shifting my glare back to Harley, I asked her, "You ready?"

"Cash." She looked at him. "I got this." Bringing her gaze back to mine, she added, "He's right though. Cash will always be in my life cuz I want him to be. *You*, only cuz our families are close. If I didn't havta see you or talk to you, I'd be livin' my best life. Don't get it twisted, I don't love you. I don't even like you. Especially now, kiss stealer. Let's get this over with. Do it so it'll be another dare I beat you at."

I smiled. "Close your eyes for me, baby girl."

Everything she said went in one ear and out the other. Her words meant nothing to me. *She* meant nothing to me. People couldn't hurt you unless you let them, and I would never let her get to me. She was just the girl...

I hated.

Harley took a deep breath and wrenched her eyes shut so tight I could see the wrinkles in the corners of her lids.

Leaning in close to her ear, where only she could hear me, I whispered, "Relax, Toots. I'm not going to hurt you. At least not right now. You'll like it. I promise."

"Like I would ever trust you, Jackson Pierce."

I grabbed onto the back of her neck and pulled her toward me. "Don't say I didn't warn you." Taking one last look at her face, I bent down to reach her mouth with mine.

She sucked in a breath, and I was struck with the smell of cherry from her lips. My pulse sped up.

What was that?

I ignored the fast-paced beating of my heart, suddenly drumming so hard I swore everyone in the shed could hear it. I went right in for the kill instead, not wanting anything or anyone to change my mind.

A split-second before my mouth touched hers, I was knocked over. Unexpectedly rammed sideways. I didn't have a choice other than to drag her with me.

I didn't have to wonder who it was.

I already knew.

Cash was going to pay for this, with my fists in his face.

He quickly yanked Harley up from the ground by her hand. "Shit! I didn't think he'd take you wit' him." Once she was fully standing, he asked her, "You alright?"

She shook away the haze, brushing him off. "I'm fine."

"If she's hurt, it's on you!" I snarled.

"You hurt her every day!"

It didn't matter there were people everywhere outside of this shed, neither one of us backed down.

I snapped.

Letting go of all my pent-up anger.

My hatred.

My frustrations.

Out on him…

"Yeah? Well I'm gonna hurt you next, McGraw!"

Without thinking twice about it, I sprang to my feet and charged him. Tackling him to the concrete.

"No!" Harley screamed, darting around us. "Get off him!"

"Stop being assholes! This isn't fixing anything!" Shiloh hollered, rushing to her cousin's side.

We didn't pay them any attention, wrestling around for a few minutes, each of us trying to gain the upper hand. Rolling around with elbows, fists, and legs flying everywhere while we brawled on the ground.

We heard the girls screaming and yelling at us to stop, like they actually expected us to.

"You're gonna get us in trouble cuz you're thinkin' with your stupid willies!" Harley shrieked. "You got nothin' to prove! I don't care who has the bigger balls! Balls are ugly! Ain't nobody want your balls!"

Cash was able to flip us over, getting on top of me. I was finally going to get a hit on his face when he was suddenly pulled back and off me.

"Cash! What the fuck?!" His dad, Dylan, reprimanded.

Harley's old man yanked me up from the ground. "Reel it in, yeah?" he ordered, holding me back as well.

"What's goin' on? You fightin' over Harley?" Dylan questioned.

"The fuck they are," Creed growled.

"No, Daddy! They ain't fightin' over me!" she explained, knowing how overprotective he was over her.

"Then why they throwin' down, baby girl?"

"Cuz Jackson started it."

"Bullshit!" I blurted. "*You.* Started it."

"Me?" She pointed to herself. "How did I start it?"

"By telling them I love you."

"The fuck?" Her daddy scoffed out, squeezing the shit out of my throwing shoulder.

"What does that havta do wit' Cash?" Dylan let out.

Harley's grandma, grandpa, and mom ran into the shed.

"What's going on?" Mia asked, her eyes scanning all of us.

I didn't give a rat's ass if I'd be in trouble, or that her old man was holding me in a death grip.

The expression on Harley's face would be worth it.

Unable to hold it in any longer, I spit fire. Booming, "You think I love you, *baby girl*? Jokes on you… I hate you. I can't stand you. I hurt you cuz I can, cuz I want to, cuz I enjoy it. You mean nothing to me. *Nothing.*"

"Ditto, asshole!"

"Harley Jameson!" her mom scolded, as her old man spun me around, seething right into my eyes.

"Daddy! Don't hurt Jackson! I got this! I'm a Jameson! We're badass motherfuckas!"

"Harley!" Mia reprimanded again, stomping her feet.

"That's what they say! I'm just repeatin' what Daddy and Uncle Noah say! Why do I get in trouble? If Daddy hurts Jackson, then he's gonna get in trouble! I'm just lookin' out for my daddy!"

"You little shit, back off before I teach you some manners. Ya feel me?"

"Oh my God! Creed!"

"Momma! It's okay, I'll teach him some manners! I got lots to teach, and he's got lots to learn!"

Out of the corner of my eye, I blinked and suddenly saw my dad stumbling out in the yard. A bottle of booze in hand, it was like he appeared out of thin air. Making me witness yet another one of my worst nightmares. Playing out in front of me. Nice and slow. For all to see.

There was nothing left of the man.

The doctor.

The father he used to be.

The one that raised me.

Loved me.

Took care of everyone.

He was as lost as my mom was.

We all were.

No one knew what was going on. We didn't even talk about it. It hurt too fucking much. His head bobbled side to side, weighing down his body. It was obvious he was shit-faced, trying to remain upright and conscious. Taking another swig from the bottle, not caring he was disgracing me.

Himself.

Our family.

It didn't even look like he knew where he was.

"What's wrong with him?" Harley muttered, never taking her eyes off my dad.

Noah quickly made his way over to him, gripping onto his arm. "Aiden, what's goin' on? Did you drive here like this?"

"Bailey…" he slurred, staggering all over the place. Barely able to stand on his own two feet.

"Jesus Christ, man!" Noah yelled at him, "What the fuck?"

He tried shoving him away, pulling another swig from his precious liquor bottle. "Bailey… Bailey… Bailey…"

Noah shook his head, grabbing onto his arm again. "For fuck's sake, Aiden."

No one, including me, had ever seen him like this. They weren't supposed to find out about my mom. Not like this.

Never. Like. This.

For the second time in the last two years, I knew my life would never be the same. When he spoke the truth, announcing to everyone, "She's gone... My Bailey... left me. Forever."

Meaning every last word.

Except it wasn't my father's face that would haunt me this time.

It was hers...

Harley's.

The girl, I hated, the most.

Chapter Eleven

Harley

My belly hurt the rest of the day, and not in an 'I ate somethin' bad kind of way. I would never forget the expression on Jackson's face when he saw his dad stumblin' around. Then again when he said Aunt Bailey was gone forever.

It was like a bullet pierced his heart and his dad was the one who pulled the trigger. It was the worst feelin' ever. I hated Jackson with every part of me, but in that moment, I felt somethin' for him I never had before.

Sadness.

I didn't understand what was goin' on. The adults made all the kids stay outside while they handled Uncle Aiden inside behind closed doors. Jackson didn't say another word to any of us, not even to his brother who looked like he felt.

Like all of us felt.

Awful and afraid.

I had so many questions with no answers.

My parents didn't speak a word on the way home. Although, at one point, my daddy reached over and grabbed my momma's hand. He kissed it before placin' it in his lap for the rest of the drive home. As if he needed to hold her any way he could.

I knew one thing for sure, whatever was happenin' in Jackson's family was really bad. Not in an *everythin' would eventually be okay* way.

"Momma, what's happenin' with Aunt Bailey?" I asked while she was cleanin' up my room as I got ready for bed.

The fact she was cleanin' my room this late only proved my point that this really was bad. Momma only cleaned this heavily when she needed a distraction.

She sighed, noddin' for me to get into bed. I did as I was told as fast as I could, wantin' to hear what she had to say. Momma swiftly sat beside me, pullin' my wet hair away from my face to look into my eyes.

"Baby, I don't think you'll understand. I barely understand it."

"But you're a grown up and adults know everythin'."

"Sweetheart, there are times in life where even adults don't understand things."

"You're scarin' me."

"Don't be scared. What I can tell you is the Pierces are a part of our family, and we'll be there for them every step of the way."

I narrowed my eyes at her, confused. "Is Aunt Bailey sick?"

She nodded. "Yeah, Harley. She's very sick."

"But Uncle Aiden is a doctor, so he can find a way to make her better, right?"

Her eyes watered. "You need to go to bed, baby. You have school in the morning."

"Is she gonna die?" I questioned, ignorin' her.

"Oh, baby…"

"Momma, I don't want her to die. She can't die, I love her. Jackson needs his momma, so does Jagger. She's everythin' to them. She's Uncle Aiden's lobster."

"I know, honey, I know," she expressed in an upset tone, bendin' over to kiss my forehead. "I love you so much, Harley. I wish I could explain this to you, but I don't have all the information yet. I promise once I know, I'll tell you. Okay?"

I nodded, feelin' an ache in my heart that wouldn't go away for nothin'. Not even her reassurin' words helped ease the pain in my chest.

For Aunt Bailey.

Uncle Aiden.

Jagger.

Jackson.

"Try to get some sleep, baby girl, yeah?" Daddy said from the door, leanin' against the frame with his arms crossed over his chest.

"I'll try."

"I love you, Harley. You're all I ever wanted. A baby girl just like you. Ya feel me?"

74

He always told me this, but tonight there was a different gleam in his eyes.

"I feel ya, Daddy. I'm pretty awesome."

He simply smiled, though he was laughin' through his stare.

Momma's eyes were waterin' from listenin' and watchin' our conversation. She always got emotional when she watched Daddy and me together. I knew it was because he was her hero too.

Leanin' in, she kissed my head one last time before turnin' the lamp off on my nightstand. Once they shut my door, I don't know how long I just laid there wide awake. My mind spinnin' over everythin' that had happened.

For the first time in my life, my parents didn't make me feel better, didn't even try. They didn't want to lie to me, and that was a hard truth to swallow.

Which only meant Aunt Bailey, Jackson's family... might not come out of this alive.

I took a deep breath at the thought and closed my eyes, tryin' to keep my tears locked inside of me. I stayed there exactly like that, hopin' this icky feelin' would go away. But for some reason I couldn't explain, I felt *him*.

Deep in my bones.

He was right there.

My eyes snapped open and my feet began to move on their own, walkin' over to the balcony off my bedroom.

My parents' room was on the other side of the house, but still, I quietly slid the doors open. Careful not to make a peep.

For the second time in a matter of seconds...

I. Felt. Him.

My heart sped up, my pulse quickened, and my feet continued to move forward.

I could see him in the moonlight, walkin' down to his dock. Except he didn't stay there. He jumped off it and went to the shoreline instead.

Holy crap! I did feel him.

Our houses weren't close to each other if you were drivin' on the roads, but on the back of our properties, we shared a huge lake.

Just do it, Harley. Go down there. Go talk to him.

I wouldn't get any sleep until I found out what was goin' on. I'd never snuck out of my house before, but at this point, I didn't have a choice. I needed answers, and the only person who could give them to me was the boy I couldn't stand.

It was him or no one.

My parents never checked on me after they shut my door for the night, but just in case, I went back to my bed and made a fake Harley with pillows. Makin' it look like I was still snoozin, safe under the covers.

Without carin' about the consequences if I got caught, I snuck out of my house. In less than a minute, I was runnin' down to my dock and grabbin' my paddle board, carefully placin' it in the water.

The lake was dead calm. You couldn't even hear a fish flappin' around. Makin' it easy to make my way over to him.

One stroke.

Ten strokes.

Thirty strokes of my paddle.

It felt as though I blinked, and I was standin' by the shoreline with him. His eyes instantly connectin' with mine. There wasn't even a hint of shock written on his face that I was right in front of him.

Almost like he knew I'd come.

Did he feel me too?

I opened my mouth to ask him what was goin' on, but he abruptly shook his head at me. Silencin' me, as if he thought I was gonna start in on him.

Did he really think I was gonna pick on him? Knowin' somethin' was up with his momma?

"Not here, Harley. Anywhere but here," he muttered, loud enough for me to hear.

I had the overwhelming urge to yell that I would never be that insensitive to him. That I would never use his hurt for whatever was goin' on with his mom against him.

That I…

That I…

That I…

Would never not care about what he was goin' through in this situation.

I may have hated him, but there was a line I wouldn't cross.

And his momma was it.

There was so much I wanted to say to him, so much he needed to know and hear. Startin' with how my family would be there for them. For him. Tell him no matter what, our hatred for one another didn't stop them from being *my* family.

I hated Jackson, but *he* was *my* boy to hate.

All mine.

"I'm sorry, Jackson. I'm so sorry about your momma," was the only thing I managed to choke out.

"So, you know? You know she has Dementia?"

I gasped, jerkin' back. I imagined it'd be bad, but I never thought it would be that bad. We just learned about dementia in school.

"Oh. My. God!"

"You fuckin' brat!" He was over to me in three strides, gettin' right in my face.

The sudden movement knocked me off my board and my butt fell hard into the water.

"I knew it!" He hovered above me like a beast, glarin' down at me with so much hate, I nearly jolted out of my skin. "I knew you'd come over here and rub it my face! What, Harley? Trying to be nosey? Want to tell me how I don't deserve a mom? How you're happy this is happening to me? How you can't wait until she's gone, so you can see me cry? See me sad, miserable, dying without her?! How much you hope I lose my mind too? That I don't remember you! Or my family! Or my life! That's what you want to say to me, right?! Tell me, baby girl! Tell me all the things you've been saving up to say to me! Tell me right now!"

"Oh my God!" I repeated with wide eyes, surrenderin' my hands out in front of me. "That's not why I came over here!"

"Bullshit! You're so full of shit! You want to hear what's going on, Nancy Drew?! You want to know how long she's been losing her shit? How she would forget her keys, her cellphone, her purse... how it started off with small things that became bigger things? Little by little, she started forgetting football games, parent-teacher conferences... dinners, meetings, dates with my dad! How we thought it was only cuz she was overwhelmed? How maybe if we would have got her checked out sooner, they could have done something? How we let it go on for an entire year when my dad is a fuckin' doctor? Tell me, Harley! Am I telling you everything you wanted to know?!"

"I'm not the enemy, Jackson! I'm here for you!"

"The fuck you aren't! You're always the enemy!"

I tried to get up. "Can you just let me—"

He loomed over me, knockin' me back down. "Did you know that my parents were trying to have the baby girl they always wanted? Did you know that maybe that could have triggered something in her mind to lose it? Huh? Tell me, smarty pants! Since you're so smart!"

I rapidly shook my head. "I didn't know that!"

His hatred-filled eyes deepened while he panted profusely, his body shaking.

"I'm sorry, Jackson! I'm so sorry!" I exclaimed, my own eyes brewin' with tears.

He'd never seen me cry. Ever, but there was no controllin' it. I'd never wanted to cry more in my life than I did in that moment with him.

Showin' him my pain.

My grief.

My support for him.

Tears slid down the sides of my face as his began to fall too. I'd never seen him cry either, only makin' this way more intense between us.

Slowly, he knelt in front of me. Gettin' so close to my face, I could feel his breath against my lips when he rasped, "You know she forgot me first? Out of everyone in her life... out of all your family, all her friends... her kids... *my mom* forgot me first."

With a stream of fresh tears, I wept, "Your mom loves you more than anythin' in this world, Jackson."

He didn't hesitate in replyin', "Sometimes... my mom doesn't even know who I am. And it's only going to get worse until she forgets me completely."

I winced, hearin' him say that was like a knife to my heart.

"The life my dad worked so hard to give her... the one he fought for... to block out all the bad memories of what happened when they were kids in the system. The life they prayed for, with their two sons and a baby girl, in the house with the white fence and red door, surrounded by sunflowers he put in the ground for her... to make her happy, to make her smile, to make her know she was loved... it doesn't matter now. None of it does. Not his struggle, not their battle to overcome all the bullshit in their way. Because in the end of her short life, she won't remember any of it, Harley. Not her, not us, no one. You want me to tell you what happens next?"

I didn't know how to respond, so I didn't say anythin'.

"Her body is going to forget how to work. She won't be able to walk, to talk, to move... until her heart forgets to beat, her lungs forget to breathe, and her body just shuts down..."

"Jackson..."

"Then, she dies. With nothing. Without even knowing she's gone and left us all behind. She lived her entire life for nothing, Harley. Do you see? Do you understand now? My mom is going to die, and then I have to spend the rest of my life wondering... waiting for the time, for the year, for the day... I'll forget everything too."

I sucked in my lips, tryin' to keep it together for him. But I couldn't help myself, I threw my arms around his neck.

Needin' him to feel my warmth.

My comfort.

My love?

It was all so confusin'. I hated him, but in that moment, it didn't feel that way.

All I could say was, "I'm so sorry, Jackson. I'm so very sorry."

He tensed in my arms, but I didn't care. I hugged him harder, tighter, showin' him I was there.

For him.

That I'd always be there for him.

Jackson

I let her hold me.

Hug me.

Be there for me...

Until I couldn't breathe. Her close presence suffocated me.

"Get off," I finally gritted through a clenched jaw.

"Jackson, please—"

"I said, get off me!"

She jumped with her arms still around my neck.

Of course, she didn't listen.

She never fuckin' listened.

I grabbed ahold of her wrists, tearing her off my body.

Looking into her eyes, I bit, "You got what you came for. Now leave before I make you."

"Jackson—"

I. Kissed. Her.

My lips smashed right into hers. I did it to shut her up. To silence her.

Right? I kissed her to make her be quiet?

Shoving those stupid thoughts away from my mind, I closed my eyes. Our mouths stayed connected for I don't know how long, time stood still. I would never tell her this, she would never know…

But it was my first kiss too.

Harley Jameson was my first kiss.

It was only to shut her up. I didn't love her. I didn't even like her. I kissed her to shut her loud ass mouth up. No other reason.

I hated her.

With those stupid thoughts again, I pulled away, leaning my forehead against hers. Quickly narrowing my gaze, I stared deep into bright blue eyes that were wide and shining.

Licking my lips, I tasted her tears. They were sweet and salty, just like her.

She was still weeping when she breathed out, "You stole my first kiss."

"No." I shook my head. "Cash did. This was my second time trying to steal it." I abruptly stood up, leaving her there.

Dazed.

Sobbing.

For me.

I always thought the first time I made her cry would be the best feeling in the world, but I was wrong. So very wrong.

I wouldn't realize this until I was much older, but Harley would eventually become my escape from the lonely life I'd create. This wouldn't be the first time she saved me.

Except, by the time I figured it out…

How much she meant to me…

It'd be too late.

Chapter Twelve

Harley

Dear Jackson "Rudolph" Pierce,

I hate u more than I did yesterday. Not only did u make me cry, u stole my first kiss. Like the ASSHOLE u are! I paddled over last night to find out what was going on with your momma, and I would never use that against u cuz I ain't evil like u.

I hope I don't get a disease from your chapped lips touching mine. I'm just glad it won't leave a scar like all the other terrible things you've done to me. For someone who has probably kissed all the girls in our whole school, U are the worst kisser EVER. I didn't enjoy it, and I won't be telling anyone u stole my first kiss.

U need more practice, cuz your lips were hard, not soft, and it hurt when you smacked them into mine. It was not romantic or a memory I will ever look back on.

In my mind, it didn't happen.

I don't cry, EVER. I just want u to know I was only crying for your momma, not for u. I don't cry for bullies, I put them to ground like my daddy.

I'm sorry this is happening to your momma. I love her. I hate it as much as I hate you, and I want ya to know that too.

U suck the biggest balls of them all, Jackson Pierce.

Not love,
Harley

P.S. I stayed up most of the night researching dementia on my laptop. Did u know u can take a test to find out if u carry the gene? Cuz u can. Not that I care if u take it or not. I'm just saying, if u wanted to, it's there. I printed out all the information for u.

P.S.S. U better not tell anyone u stole my first kiss, or I'll kick your big sucky balls really hard and u won't be able to walk right for the entire week.

I HATE YOU.

Jackson

April 25th

April 25th

Dear Harley "Gremlin" Jameson,

U should have never come over last night. I didn't want or need u there. I only kissed u to shut your loud ass mouth up. I wasn't trying to be romantic, and if u want to pretend like it didn't happen, then I will just have to kiss u over and over until u remember it. Cuz now it's just another thing of yours that belongs to me.

The best part of last night was finally seeing u cry. I can't wait to do it again. Try to kick me in my balls and watch how fast I stick my tongue down your throat. I'll make sure to eat lots of onions and pickles before too, so you can taste my hatred for u.

Get used to it, Harley. I win. Forever.

With all my hate for u,
Jackson

P.S. Mind your own business. I don't need u researching anything for me. U really are stupid if u think I'm going to read all that information. All u did was kill a bunch of trees. I have better things to do than listen to a baby girl who is as dumb as she looks.

P.S.S. I already told the football team I stole your first kiss, and the whole school will know by the end of the day. U are mine to hurt and play with. No one else's. Mine. Not even your stupid Cash McGraw can keep u from me. By the time u read this, your dumbass friends will know it too. I hope Cash realizes that I win, and he loses, always.

I'm the boss.

I. Own. You.

AND I HATE YOU MORE.

Harley

10-11

Dear Jackson "Asshole" Pierce,

I hate u more today than I did yesterday.

It's been six months since I found out about your momma. I just wanna know how she's doing. Can u at least give me that? Aunt Skyler says she's having more good days than bad. That makes me happy for her and your family.

I don't feel bad I kicked u in the nuts yesterday, cuz u deserved it for being a shithead. I told u I didn't want to go swimming in the lake, cuz I just got my hair blow dried by a professional for my birthday party and u didn't listen or care. Your balls paid the price. I hope u felt them in your stomach. I noticed u couldn't walk right all day.

You're welcome. ☺

I can't wait to do it again.

Not love,
Harley

P.S. If u try to stick your tongue down my throat again, I will tell the whole school u gave me mono and no one will ever kiss you again.

P.S.S. I found more research on the genetic testing and I printed it out for u. I think u should do it. Not cuz I care, but I think it would give your daddy some peace of mind. Do it for him.

I still hate u.

Jackson

October 12th

Dear Harley "Nosey Ass" Jameson,

How many times do I have to tell u to mind your own business? My mom is not your concern. I don't want to talk about it, especially with u.

It's been six months since I stole your first kiss, and I've kissed u seven times since. Only because u keep kicking me in my balls. U do it so I will kiss u. I'm not brainless like u are.

And guess what, Toots? One day I will stick my tongue down your throat, u can't hold it shut forever. I'll make my way in, and then you'll be more obsessed with me than u already are.

Besides, u should be thanking me. I pushed u in the lake to do u a favor. U looked weirder than u normally do. U don't need your hair professionally done and u don't need makeup, cuz u can't fix ugly.

You're welcome. ☺

With all my hate for u,
Jackson

P.S. Your threats mean nothing to me. Tell the school what u want. I'm the quarterback. This town loves me. Including all the girls. They will probably stand in line just so they can say Jackson Pierce gave them mono too.

P.S.S. No amount of research will make me read that information. Stop killing trees, Harley. U don't know anything, especially what my dad feels.

I still hate u more.

$$Harley$$

7-4

Dear Jackson "The Most Stubborn Boy" Pierce,

There's a dog at the animal shelter I'm volunteering at this summer, and he reminds me of u. He's dumb as rocks and eats his own poo. I named him Rudolph cuz he looks exactly like u. Big elf ears and a button nose. He acts like u too. He drools, smells bad, farts, and makes grunting noises when he doesn't get his way.

85

See, it's like I'm talking about u.

He thinks he's alpha of the pack, and it doesn't matter how many times I tell him not to be a jerk, he doesn't listen.

It's like u guys are twins.

He bit me yesterday cuz I told him no. Sounds familiar, right? I knew you'd agree.

I hope u liked the pink polish I painted on your nails while u were sleeping at the clubhouse this weekend. I think pink is really your color. U should have never dumped my purse on the ground and stepped on all my makeup and my new Jackson Blockers.

I don't even feel bad I left Rudolph's poo under your mattress. Jagger said u couldn't figure out where the shit smell was coming from...

It came from me.

You're welcome.

Not love,
Harley

P.S. It's been over a year since u stole my first kiss, and I've decided I'm going to kiss Brody at the 4th of July Festival tonight. HE will officially be my FIRST KISS.

Not u.

P.S.S. I can't wait to kiss him. He likes me, maybe even loves me. He might be my lobster. And I WILL let him stick his tongue down my throat.

P.S.S.S. I overheard your daddy talking to Uncle Noah about how he fucked up. His words, not mine. He said your momma was right there and he hadn't been with her in months... I don't understand, but now your momma wants to keep it cuz it will complete your family like they always wanted.

Are you getting a dog? If so, adopt, don't shop.

Jackson

Dear Harley "Turd Burglar" Jameson,

It sounds like u are finally with your real family. A bunch of stinky ass mutts who don't know how to control themselves. I hope Rudolph bit u nice and hard. Maybe now you'll catch rabies and it will fix what's wrong with u.

Again, I did you a favor. When are u going to thank me? I'm just looking out for the people who have to stare at u wearing makeup, Gremlin. You remember Greta the Gremlin? Well, she looks way better with makeup on than u do.

As for the Jackson Blockers, that was just an added bonus.

By the way, you missed a great time last night at the festival. Sucks your daddy didn't let u come out. Shiloh said u didn't understand how your old man found out Brody "likes" u.

It came from me.

You're so welcome.

With all my hate for u,
Jackson

P.S. It doesn't matter how many times u tell me I wasn't your first kiss. I was and there's nothing u can do to change that.

P.S.S. Brody's tongue was definitely deep down into Dixie's throat. He was getting all up in there. I heard they went to second base. Since u don't even have boobs, I can see why he went for someone who actually looks like a girl.

P.S.S.S. MIND YOUR OWN DAMN BUSINESS.

If I ever do get a dog, it will be purebred and bought from a private breeder. Why? Cuz they're better. Just like I am compared to u.

2-24

Dear Jackson "I still hate you" Pierce,

Congratulations on your new baby sister.

I know it was really hard on your mom and family to have her, but babies are always a blessing. It was what your mom wanted too. Even though the doctors, the specialists, and your daddy said it wasn't a good idea, she wanted to complete your family.

It's what mommas do. Their kids always come first, no matter what, and your mom is no different. Aunt Skyler told me your momma said she wanted to leave your daddy with the kids they always wanted. The baby girl they always dreamt about. She thinks God wanted it that way too.

I'm telling u this cuz I know you're upset Journey's birth is making your mom leave faster, but it's not her fault. It's not even your dad's. It was her choice, Jackson. I saw how much she fought everyone on it. There was no telling her she wasn't having your baby sister.

Your parents are lobsters. They love each other like Beauty and the Beast. They will forever be soulmates. In case u didn't know, it's true. It don't matter if she's alive or gone, she will always live in everyone's hearts.

Please don't forget that.

I love the name Journey. I got to hold her yesterday. She's the third baby I've ever held, other than my brothers. She's so tiny and smells so good. I don't know how she is related to u, cuz she's awesome and u suck so bad.

I want u to know I still hate u with all my heart and soul. U are evil to the core, Jackson Pierce. But if u ever need someone to talk to or yell at again... I'm here.

Just don't make me cry or else I'll teach Journey how to kick u in the nuts, and then u will have two girls that own your balls.

Not love,
Harley

P.S. Your mom is in my thoughts and prayers.

For the first time in over two years, Jackson didn't write me back. I didn't realize this until I was older, but what happened next in his life, changed him in ways I never saw comin'.

He went from the boy I always hated, to the guy I'd eventually...

Fall head over heels in love with.

Chapter Thirteen

Jackson

Then: Twelve years old

With my brother, our father, and my one-month-old baby sister in my arms, we walked toward the room that had become a home to the woman I know longer knew. There was nothing left of *my* mother, *our* mother, *his* wife.

Journey had taken it all.

I held her tighter, needing her now more than ever before.

The entire time my mom was pregnant, I hated Journey just as much as I did Harley.

However, the second I saw her sleeping in the hospital nursery, I was slapped in the face with the amount of love I immediately felt for her. Except it wasn't until she was placed against my chest that I felt, that I saw, that I knew...

My mother would live on through her.

Journey Pierce was her legacy, and I instantly understood why she was so adamant about having her. She completed our family, when my mom was tearing it apart.

No warmth.

No happiness.

No mother of our own.

The hallway was long and narrow, making it feel as if we were walking death row. I guess in a way, we were. Nothing would be the same after this.

Not our future.

Not our lives.

Not our hearts.

This was our demise.

Our final goodbye.

To a woman who had already mentally died a few days after giving birth.

Words, tears, feelings wouldn't change the outcome, and I refused to admit the woman lying there was my mother. She wouldn't want me to remember her that way. Unrecognizable, a frail person wasting away to nothing as her body began to shut itself down. I had to remember I was doing this for Journey, she deserved to see her one last time.

Although, it was killing me inside.

Each step, each stride, each minute that passed, I lost more and more air, more and more will, more and more life.

Every last part of me hurt, throbbed, ached.

I was there, but I wasn't.

Possibly losing my mind as well.

My father showed no emotion like a patron of strength, but he didn't fool me. I knew this was his very worst nightmare playing out in front of him. My mother was his everything.

He would have switched places with her in a second if he could. I knew his truth like I still knew my own name.

How much time did I have? When was I going to lose my memory and end up here too?

Never ending questions ran heavy through my head, feeling an intense amount of fear.

For me.

For her.

For my family.

The closer we got to her room, the clearer the ending became for all of us in the exact same way.

Bile rose in the back of my throat, but I swallowed it down.

I just kept moving, kept stepping, kept going forward. There was nothing left behind me. Only memories gradually fading away the closer we got to her.

Seeing her face.

Hearing her voice.

Feeling her love.

Was what helped me go through with this.

"Jackson, my golden boy. You're the best thing that's ever happened to me. Do you know that? Do you know how much I love you? You're my baby boy. You'll always be my baby boy."

Memory after memory attacked my mind.

"I'm so proud of you. You're just like your daddy. Out of both of my boys, you're the most like your daddy."

Her love for me flashed before my eyes.

"You can do whatever you set your mind to, Jackson. You want to be a football star, a surgeon, walk on the moon... you can do it. Because you're the smartest boy with the brightest of futures. Don't you ever forget that."

The good...

"I will always be here for you."

The bad...

"I don't know why this is happening, baby. I wish I could tell you. I wish I had answers, but I don't. All I can say is live your life, Jackson. You live your life like nothing happened to me. Do you hear me? Are you listening? I need you to be free from me. You live. You love. You laugh. You be happy. No matter the outcome."

The ugly...

"I don't know who you are! I hate you! I never want to see you again! I'm not your mom! I'm not your anything!"

Each memory was worse than the last.

"Get him out of my room! Leave and never come back! Who are you? What do you want with me? I have no sons. I have no family!"

To the last memory I had of her before I lost her completely.

"You look good holding your baby sister, Jackson. I can already tell she is going to have you wrapped around her little finger."

"Mmm hmm..."

"Baby, please look at me. Please..."

I shook my head. *"I can't."*

"Why?"

"Cause it always takes you away from me."

"Oh, Jackson..."

She tugged me into her arms, holding onto us so tightly. I never wanted to leave her side. This would be the last time she'd ever hold me. The last hug I'd ever receive from anyone. I'd never let another person get that close to me.

"I love you, baby. I love you so much. Please tell me you know that."

"Mmm hmm…"

"Promise me you know I'll always live in your heart."

I didn't say a word.

"Promise me."

"Which one of you? The woman who raised me, or the woman who doesn't remember me?"

She burst into tears. "I'm sorry," she wept. "I'm so sorry for everything I have ever said or done to you. It's not me. I swear to you, it's not me."

I pulled away, looking deep into her eyes. "I don't know who you are anymore. I can't even call you my mother cuz it's your biggest trigger. You lose it on me every time."

I could seet through her gaze she knew I was right.

She simply stated, "I love you. You'll always be my baby boy with bright blue eyes. You're going to be like your daddy, never like me."

"You don't know that."

"Take the test, Jackson. Take it for your own peace of mind."

"I can't."

"Why?"

"Because I'm not ready to give up on my life yet."

"Dr. Pierce," the physician said to my dad, ripping me back to the present place and time. "She doesn't have much time left. Her organs are completely shutting down."

I saw it, clear as day.

Our father wanted to die right along with her.

"Her dementia has completely taken over. I'm so sorry, Dr. Pierce," the nurse informed him, breaking his heart all over again.

It didn't matter how many times someone talked about her illness, it was like a bullet to the soul each and every time.

How could he go on without her?

When all he did was live for her.

In a neutral tone, he stated, "You guys can go in first."

We both nodded, staying strong for our father. When all we wanted to do was fall apart with him.

As soon as she saw us walking through the door, she smiled weakly, taking us in. It was evident in her tired eyes she had no idea who we were.

"Hey, Bailey," Jagger greeted, barely keeping it together.

He wasn't as strong as me and Dad were, I knew he was going to lose his shit. It was only a matter of time before he couldn't keep it in any longer.

I didn't say one word. I don't even think I was breathing while I looked at her with so much love and so much hate all at once.

"You look really pretty today. Do you want me to brush your hair?" my brother asked.

She didn't say anything, didn't even move. There were very few words she could still say. The dementia had almost completely taken away her speech. She was lost within herself, staring off into space where we were no longer her escape.

"Can we take a picture with you?" Jagger asked, tears swelling up in his eyes.

Out of nowhere, I blurted, "She can't talk to you. She doesn't even know who the fuck we are. She doesn't even know we're here."

"Jackson," Dad gritted.

"What?" I snapped my eyes over to him. "It's the truth. Why are we even here? This is fucking pointless."

"Jackson, just cut Dad a break. It's not his fault this happened. It's not even hers," Jagger stressed, pointing to her.

"I guess we should try to remember that. Oh wait…" I mocked. "We may not have our memory in a few years either."

There was nothing anyone could say to that. It was our reality and truth.

"Can we just take a picture? Journey deserves to have one photo with mom."

"Yeah, whatever." I rolled my eyes, clenching my jaw. Trying to keep my shit together. "We can pretend she gives a rat's ass about us."

"Jesus, Jackson! Can you just stop? For our sister's sake?"

I was so angry…

At her.

At my dad.

At the fucking world.

They couldn't help me. They couldn't even help themselves.

Jagger leaned in with his phone out in front of him, and I followed his lead with Journey still in my arms as he quickly snapped a photo. But unlike me, Jagger stayed next to her.

I didn't want to touch her.

See her.

Or feel her.

It hurt too damn much.

Dad and I watched as Jagger bent over to kiss her head, letting his lips linger for a few seconds.

With tears streaming down his face, he whispered something in her ear that made her blink and shut her eyes as he continued to privately have a moment with her.

I shook my head, angrily scoffing out, "Fuck this." In two strides, I was walking out of the room with Journey on my hip, but Dad grabbed my free arm, stopping me.

"I know you're angry," he voiced, staring into my eyes. "I understand, alright? But you don't want to do this. Trust me, Jackson, if you walk out of here and you don't say goodbye to your mom, it's going to haunt you forever. And I don't want that for you. Please, son, say goodbye to your mother."

"Don't you get it? She's not here to say goodbye to. There's nothing left of the woman who loved me, raised me, told me she'd always be here for me. She's already gone!" I roared, tearing my arm out of his grasp, nodding over to her bed.

My glare.

My rage.

Stayed consumed on her, wanting to look at her one last time.

This was the moment I'd look back on later and deeply regret. If I knew then what I knew now, I would have hugged her, showed her how much I loved her, told her how much she meant to me, how much she would always mean to me.

All it took was one decision to change the course of my life. One choice to fuck it all up. This was a life sentence for me.

I put the nail in my own coffin that day.

I didn't say goodbye to my mother, not realizing I'd never get a second chance to make it right.

Allowing my emotions to get the best of me, I spoke with conviction, "That's not my mom. I don't know who that is." Before I could change my mind, I abruptly turned and left them there. Barely making it around the corner before I laid my back and head against the cool tiled wall. Needing the support to hold me and my baby sister up as I overheard Jagger bawling his eyes out to our father.

"Shhh…" Dad muttered. "Shhh… I got you, Son. I got you."

Who's going to hold me? Who has me?

"Why is this happening? Why, Dad, why?"

"I wish I knew, Jagger. I wish I knew."

"Where is she going to go? You know she hates being alone, Dad," he sobbed. "She hates it so much."

She does hate it. Who's going to protect her now? When she's really alone.

"Shhh... it's alright... it's okay... look, Journey needs you to be strong. Be the strong boy we raised."

He sucked in breaths and I looked down at Journey who was wide awake, peering up at me. She had no idea what was going on. Her eyes reminding me so much of my mom's.

"She's going to a better place, where she won't be in any pain. Where she still knows who she is and can watch over you," Dad lied. He didn't know that.

No one did.

"You promise?" Jagger questioned, but I didn't hear his response.

Why? Because he knew it was a lie as well.

"I love you, Dad."

"I love you too, Jagger. You, Jackson, and Journey were all we ever wanted. I swear to you."

Jagger took a deep, long breath, catching his bearings before I saw him walk down the hall. Leaving Dad alone with what was left of his wife.

His Beauty.

His whole world was in that room.

I blinked and I was once again standing by the door to her room. Witnessing him sitting on the edge of her bed, he grabbed her hand.

And for the first time in my life...

I watched my hero, lose his battle. The war to let her go.

He hunched over, laying his head on top of her chest and broke the fuck down. Crying like a newborn baby. My chest pounded and my throat burned, feeling all his love and devotion for her.

He sucked in air that wasn't available for the taking.

Tears slid out of my eyes, scared for him.

For her.

For us.

When her hand started lazily rubbing his back, we both suddenly froze. "Beauty?" he rasped, pulling away to look into her eyes.

There was no expression on her face, no recollection in her stare, but still it felt like she might be there with him.

"I'm tiiiirrrreeedd."

He caressed her pale cheek, "I know, baby, I know."

"Sllleeeeepppp noooooowwwww."

I shut my eyes, I had to. My chest was caving in on me. My world

96

crumbling down on me.

In two seconds flat, I was leaning against the wall again, except this time I was sliding down it, holding Journey firmly against my broken heart.

Unable to hold myself up any longer.

"Beeeeee heeeeerrrrreeee," were the last words I ever heard her say.

"I'll always be here for you, Bailey. No matter what. It's always going to be me and you against the world, Bay. Always."

I stayed right there.

I didn't move an inch.

Until she took her last breath.

Until all the machines around her went crazy.

Until she passed away…

But it wasn't until I heard my father murmur, "Take me with you, Bay… please, just take me with you."

That I realized I felt the same way.

Chapter Fourteen

Harley

Then: Eleven years old

"Would anyone else like to say anything?" the minister asked at Aunt Bailey's funeral.

I stood up in the pew and everyone's eyes turned toward me. Patting down the sides of my black dress, I nodded.

My eyes quickly connected with Jackson's stare, who was sittin' in the front pew, four rows ahead of where my family was seated. Swiftly, I made my way up to the podium down the side aisle of the silent church. The only sound was the clickin' of my heels clackin' away underneath me, echoin' with the rhythm of my fast beatin' heart.

I only had one shot at this, I didn't wanna mess it up. Once I was standin' in front of everyone, I took a deep breath, peerin' out over the crowd of tear-soaked faces. Tryin' to gather my thoughts about what I wanted to say. I didn't really think this through, all I knew was I had to say somethin'.

For him.

The boy I still hated the most.

Jackson's dry eyes narrowed in on me, waitin', anticipatin' what I possibly had to say at a time like this. I had yet to see him cry, to grieve the loss of the most important person in his life while he sat there holdin' his baby sister next to Jagger who was a mess. Even after all the kind words everyone was expressin' about his momma to God and the church filled to the brim with people, he hadn't shed one tear.

With my stare directed solely on him, I spoke from the heart. "I've known Aunt Bailey since the day I was born. She ain't blood related, but that didn't matter. She was my aunt. The Pierces are our family."

Jackson held his head up higher, still only focused on me with a blank expression on his face. In that moment, I couldn't help but notice his black suit made him appear older. He didn't look like the boy I'd known all my life. More like the man that just lost his mother.

Out of the corner of my eye, I saw my momma and daddy noddin' for me to continue.

"Aunt Bailey was one of a kind. She was beautiful, graceful, smart. Her smile lit up a room, her laugh was contagious, and she always smelled like fresh sunflowers. She was one of the strongest women I've ever known. Her love and devotion for her family, her friends, her husband and kids were inspirin'. She was a second mom to us all, it's just who she was." I shrugged. "One of the best memories I have with her was when I spent the night at her house cuz Momma was havin' my baby brother Owen at the hospital. The nightlight I brought with me from my room broke," I half told the truth.

Jackson broke it, but I didn't think it was the right time to remind everyone how much he sucked.

"The guest bedroom I was sleepin' in was super dark, and I swear I could hear voices. After findin' the courage to run outta the room, I ran straight to Aunt Bailey's bedroom. Knockin' so hard on the door, I'm surprised it didn't fall off the hinges. You see, I hate the dark. Even to this day, I'm terrified of dark rooms. I don't go in them, I don't sleep in them, to me they don't exist."

Jackson knew that. *Why?* Cuz Jackson knew everythin' about me. He made it a point, so he could torture me.

"When Aunt Bailey opened the door, I jumped into her arms. Wrappin' them so hard around her, I don't think she could breathe." I chuckled, rememberin' how she instantly hugged me back.

Jackson's eyes still hadn't left my face, as if he was relivin' that time with me.

"I had a meltdown, blabberin' all sorts of things about monsters and Freddy Krueger, and the dude that lives under the bed who's always tryin' to get me."

Everyone laughed, and I smiled rememberin' the night like it happened yesterday and not years ago.

"Aunt Bailey didn't make me feel like I was a sissy or a scaredy cat. She told me she was afraid of the dark too. We walked back to my room together, and she stayed with me the whole night, rubbin' my back and my hair. When I woke up the next mornin', not only was she still with me, Jackson and Jagger were in the bed as well."

I think I saw Jackson's eyes water, but as quickly as the tears appeared, he blinked them away. Makin' me think I imagined it.

"That was the power of Aunt Bailey's love," I went on. "It brought people together, naturally gravitatin' to her. Even if they hated each other."

Everyone was cryin', while I was strugglin' to hold back the tears, bowin' my head to keep them from comin' out.

"That's just the kind of woman she was. And I'm gonna miss her very much. She will forever live in my heart, and I know she would be happy we're celebratin' her life today and not mournin' her death." I steadied my composure before I looked back up.

Lockin' eyes with Jackson again.

His stare never left my face as I made my way over to his father. I wrapped my arms around him, wantin' him to feel my sadness for them.

Uncle Aiden kissed the top of my head, whisperin', "Bailey always said she wanted a baby girl just like you. Journey has big shoes to fill, Harley."

I hugged him tighter, and Jagger joined in. Jackson didn't move from the place he was sittin'.

Mouthin', "*I still hate you.*"

I paid him no mind, goin' back to my seat instead. Daddy pulled me into his strong embrace, kissin' the top of my head too.

He drawled, "Proud of you, baby."

I smiled up at him, and then we continued listenin' as several people shared a lovin' memory of Aunt Bailey. Uncle Aiden, Uncle Noah, Aunt Skyler, Jagger…

While Jackson still didn't say a word.

For the rest of the memorial, he just sat there, no expression on his face, no sentiment in his eyes, no emotion whatsoever. Almost like he wasn't even there.

"Is Jackson going to be okay?" I asked, walkin' into the Pierces' kitchen later that evenin'.

We'd spent the rest of the day at their home, surrounded by family. Tryin' to be there for them anyway we could.

Although, from the second Jackson stepped foot in his house, he went straight to his bedroom and didn't come out. Even when Uncle Noah went in there to check on him. He was also havin' a hard time with Bailey's death, seein' as she was like a second mother to him.

This wasn't easy on anyone.

She was a pivotal person to so many people.

The expression on Momma's face didn't reassure me in the least.

"He will be, baby, with time."

"The funeral was beautiful today. I think Aunt Bailey would have loved it. Especially all the sunflowers we laid her to rest with at the cemetery."

Aunt Skyler agreed, "I think so too, Harley." She gleamed at me. "You did a great job on your eulogy, honey. Uncle Noah was very proud of you."

"I tried to say what I was feelin'."

"Those always make for the best speeches."

Out of nowhere, I saw somethin' fall from the roof.

Was that a cup?

I backed away, unnoticed. Before I knew what I was doin' or where I was standin', I was at Jackson's bedroom door.

"Jackson?" I called out, knockin' softly.

No answer.

"Jackson, you in there?"

Still, no answer.

My hand turned the knob and I peeked one eye into his space, in case he was...

I don't know, naked.

Ain't nobody wanna see that.

"Where are you?" I said to myself, findin' his bedroom empty.

It smelled like a giant butthole.

How do boys live like this?

There was a mess everywhere—shoes, clothes, football equipment, even the suit jacket he was wearin' today—on his unmade bed.

I walked around as though a bomb was about to go off, keepin' my eyes peeled for booby traps along the way. Trust me, if he found me in his room, he'd explode in my face.

Lookin' out the window next, I searched for him through the darkness.

"Jackson?"

"Holy shit, you really are Nancy Drew."

I jumped out of my skin, hittin' my head on the window rail. "Ow!"

"Serves you right for snooping."

101

Followin' the sound of his voice, I found him sittin' on the roof. His collared shirt was halfway unbuttoned, and his tie hung loosely around his neck. His hair was ruffled up like he'd been pullin' at it, yet it was his eyes that shocked me the most.

He'd been cryin'.

Was that why he was up there by himself?

"You've been cryin'," I blurted what I was thinkin'.

"No shit, Captain Obvious."

"Umm... should I... I mean... do you—"

"No, nosey ass, you're already standin' there. Just come up here."

"How?"

"I thought Harley could do anything I could do."

I glared at him, and he nodded toward the tree branch above my head.

"I'm wearin' a dress."

"It isn't anything I haven't seen before. Remember? Bath time?"

"We were like two."

"And there's photographic evidence."

"You're a creeper."

"Considering your body still hasn't changed since then, there isn't much to see."

I glared at him again, and he rolled his eyes at me, reachin' for my hand.

I bit my lip, debatin'.

"What's wrong, baby girl? Don't trust me?"

I sighed, givin' in. "If you let go of my hand, Jackson Pierce, I will forever hate you."

He grinned. "Harley, don't tempt me." Further leanin' toward me, he instructed, "Step on the windowsill and grab my hand. I'll take care of the rest."

"You can't carry me up there."

"I carry guys four times your weight in football. Now are you gonna listen, or just continue being a pain in my ass?"

"Fine, but I swear—"

"Yeah, yeah, yeah... I got it. Come on."

I did as I was told, and he kept up his end of the bargain. In less than a few seconds, he was draggin' me up on the roof as if I weighed nothin'.

"Huh, you are strong. Who woulda thought?" I peered around. "Wow. It's beautiful up here."

"I've been coming up here since I could walk."

"I always knew you were adopted from the zoo."

"I used to come up here so much, my mom had to install a security lock so I couldn't climb out here anymore."

"Maybe your real family is a pack of gorillas?" I nodded. "It makes sense."

"Sit down before I throw you off, Gremlin," he ordered in a teasin' tone.

I nodded again, sittin' right beside him.

"So... whataya doin' up here?"

"Thinking."

"About?"

He didn't think twice about it, spewin'

"How much I hate you."

Chapter Fifteen

Harley

"Nothin' new. What else?" I retorted, unfazed by his words.

"Life."

"What about it?"

"Did you come up here to be Chatty Kathy?"

I shrugged. "Maybe you need someone to talk to."

"Someone? Or *you*?"

"Does it matter?"

"Not right now."

"Jackson, I know we hate each other, but that don't change the fact I'm a good listener. I don't need to talk."

"What do you want me to say, Harley?"

"I don't know. You're up here cryin' by yourself, so you obviously got a lot to say."

He narrowed his eyes at me, archin' an eyebrow. "The night you ran to my mom's room, the voices you thought you heard, was *me*. I put a walkie talkie under the mattress."

My mouth dropped open and I punched him in the arm.

"You hit like a girl."

I punched him again. "You dick! I haven't been able to sleep in that room since."

"I didn't want you to sleep here in the first place."

"Whatever. You were sleepin' next to me when I woke up."

"That's cuz you're a bed hog. There was nowhere else to go."

"Then why were you in there, if you didn't want me here?"

Not answerin' my question, his gaze shifted upward as he leaned back. Layin' completely down on the roof. I didn't wait long to join him.

We stared up at the star-speckled sky, the moon shinin' down on us, for I don't know how long. I was surprised it wasn't awkward between us like I thought it would be. Not that I was thinkin' about bein' alone with him or anythin'. The silence was comfortin', probably cuz Jackson wasn't openin' his loud ass mouth and bein' the bully he always was to me.

It felt… natural.

I lightly gasped when I felt his rough fingers press against mine, ever so slightly.

"School was one of the most important things to her, and she's not even going to see me graduate. Take me to college like all the other annoying parents dropping off their kids. Crying that their babies are all grown up. I can picture it in my head, her standing there, waving goodbye with tears in her eyes, but it won't ever happen for me. She's gone and she's not coming back," he paused, collectin' his thoughts. "Journey won't remember her at all. Not her smell, not her touch, not the sound of her laughter or voice. She won't even know her smile."

"It always lit up a room," I chimed in, tryin' to ignore his calloused fingers startin' to caress the back of my hand.

What was happenin'?

"I guess I should feel lucky I got the time I did with her, but I'm not. I'm fuckin' pissed. I feel like I've been cheated. Like God's playing some cruel joke on me for being so bad. What's that saying? Karma's a bitch? It's not fair. None of this is fuckin' fair."

"You're right. It's not fuckin' fair. No one deserves this. Not even you, Jackson."

His fingers entwined with mine, and before I knew it, he was holdin' my hand. I swallowed hard, pretendin' like his touch wasn't affectin' me.

Why was he holdin' my hand?

"You didn't have to go up there today and share that memory, but I'd be lying if I said I wasn't glad you did. I'd forgotten about that night. Over the last five years, I feel like I've forgotten about a lot of things and it makes me think I'm losing my mind too."

My eyes widened. His words stunned me in ways I never expected. This was the most he'd ever spoken to me about anythin' personal. A huge part of me wanted him to continue lettin' me in. I laid there in awe, just waitin' for him to say more.

Why did I want him to let me in? I hated him.

"I don't want to lose my mind, Harley. I don't want to be like her," he whispered, so low I could barely hear him. "She's my mother, the woman who gave me life, and I want to be nothing like her. Do you have any idea how hard that is?"

"You can take the test—"

He squeezed my hand. "Don't."

Turnin' my head, I peered at the side of his face. Changin' the subject, I asked him, "Jackson, why are ya holdin' my hand?"

Our eyes locked when he turned his head, grinnin', "You're holding my hand."

"You held mine first."

"I like takin' your firsts, Harley."

"Why?"

"Why not?"

My eyebrows lowered, starin' at him intensely. "Do you like me?"

"Do you want me to like you?"

"No."

"No?"

"Are you messin' with me right now?"

"Does it feel like I am?"

"You ain't answerin' any of my questions."

"You aren't answering any of mine."

Why are boys so weird?

"What's that?"

"What's what?"

"That." He nodded to the pin on my dress.

"Oh. Umm… your mom gave it to me."

He hastily sat up, lettin' go of my hand in the process, and I instantly felt the loss of his warmth.

I jerked back when his hands went for my chest. "What are you doin'?"

"Relax, Gremlin. I'm not trying to touch your boobies. You don't have any."

"I hate y—"

He was goin' for the pin, fumblin' around. He unlocked it and took it off me.

"Hey! That's mine!"

"No, actually it's mine."

"Nuh uh, your mom gave it to me."

106

"It wasn't hers to give."

"Jackson, it's a Harley with a sunflower on it. I'm the Harley, and she's the sunflower."

"No, the Harley signifies adventure with the sunflower being my mom. Meaning my mom would be along for the ride with me. She gave this to me years ago."

"Well, she gave it to me last year."

"What else has she given you?"

I frowned at his question, but immediately tried to hide it.

"What was that?"

"What?" I reached for the pin, ignornin' his question to the sudden change in my expression. He lifted his arm up higher and away from me. "Give it back."

"Not a chance."

"It's mine!"

"Not anymore."

"Jacks—"

"What else has my mom given you?"

"Ugh! Fine! I'll just take it!" With that, I tackled him, but it only lasted for a second. He effortlessly flipped us, and my back hit the shingles with a hard thud.

Ouch.

Now, he was layin' on top of me.

Holdin' me completely captive.

Jackson

Why wouldn't she answer my question? What was she hiding?

I've always been impulsive.

Never thinking about the consequences to my actions.

I went with what I was feeling, always.

Going straight to what would drive her wild, I tickled her ribs. She thrashed around, screaming and laughing all at the same time.

"Shhh…" I ordered. "Hush up, or people are going to hear you."

"Then stop torturin' me!"

"I said, shhh…"

I sat on her thighs and gripped her wrists, placing them above her head. She whipped around a few more times to no avail before finally giving up, laughing too hard to fight.

I laughed too.

The sound was contagious.

I couldn't remember the last time I'd laughed, and that thought alone made me think I was losing my mind all over again.

We both found our bearings, and it was then I realized our current position. By the look in her eyes, she did too.

I peered down at her while she was gazing up at me with a look I couldn't quite read. I knew everything about Harley, from what pissed her off, to what made her happy. I didn't recognize the emotion behind her eyes, and it was the first time I witnessed her guard toward me wholeheartedly crumbling down.

Like an avalanche, fast and furious.

My hand slid toward her cheek, brushing her hair away so I could see her face.

I didn't know what the hell was happening to me. What was going on with me, but in that moment, in that second, I wanted to steal her happiness away. I wanted it to be mine.

It was just another thing that belonged to me.

All of her. Mine.

Allowing my sudden urges to take control, overpowering all rationality, my fingers started caressing the side of her face. I had no idea what message this was sending, other than she was mine to play with.

I couldn't help myself.

I grabbed the back of her neck, bringing her up to me. Her bright blue eyes were wide as saucers as my lips touched hers. They were just as I remembered, and for that reason alone, it made me feel beyond thankful I memorized the feel of her mouth against mine.

I wasn't losing my mind, at least not when it came to her.

This kiss was much different than our last.

I wanted to feel her lips in a much different way than I had when we were younger. Slowly, I opened my mouth as she sucked in a breath, caught off guard as much as I was from me taking it this far.

Her lips were so soft, and it was the craziest sensation I'd ever felt. I hadn't kissed anyone else since her. The rumors at school were only that—*rumors*. With everything that was going on in my life, girls were the last thing on my mind.

She was so tense beneath me that I found myself murmuring,

"Relax, baby girl, and open your mouth for me."

She hesitated with a confused expression on her face.

"Please, Harley…"

Acknowledging the desperation in my voice, her lips parted in the same rhythm as mine. It was the most overwhelming feeling I'd ever experienced. When my tongue slid into her mouth, I tasted chocolate cake and vanilla coke.

If I thought I'd hated her before, well this just added a whole new element and spin on it.

In those minutes, I didn't care because…

She was making me feel something other than the sadness that had consumed my whole life these last few years.

I didn't know it then, but this was when I began to rely on her for more than just pranks and fights. This was when things took an unexpected turn for the future.

This was when…

She went from the girl I hated the most, to the one I needed more than anything in this world.

I sought out her tongue again, tangling it with mine.

This kiss was slow and sloppy.

Hot and cold.

Familiar yet unknown.

Both my hands found the sides of her face, and I kissed her harder, deeper. Enjoying every second of it before I pecked her puffy lips one last time.

Leaning my forehead against hers, inches away from her mouth, I opened my eyes to find hers already open. Like she never closed them to begin with. They were dark and dilated, luring me into her heated gaze.

Neither one of us said anything, not a word, but I was the first to break the silence.

Throwing her words back in her face, I rasped, "Still want to bite off my tongue, Harley?"

She didn't respond, which was very unlike her.

"I didn't steal anything this time, you gave it to me. This pin though." I showed it to her. "This, I'm taking back."

Still, she said nothing.

I should have known better.

I should have seen it coming.

Nope.

Her leg flew up and kneed me in the balls so hard, I toppled over while she shoved me off her.

"That's fucking cheating, Harley!"

"I didn't give you anythin'! Real kiss stealer!"

"Who were you gonna kiss anyway? I just did you a favor."

"I told you not to mess with me. See what happens when you don't listen."

"Gremlin, I can't even see straight right now," I groaned, rolling onto my back.

"Good, then maybe you'll leave me alone. Serves you right for not only stealin' my first kiss, but my real first kiss too. You're a thief. It didn't belong to you!"

"Don't act like you didn't want it."

"Don't flatter yourself, Rudolph."

"I'm just speaking the truth."

She snatched the pin out of my hand. "This is mine. Not yours. Mine!"

"You better run and hide, Harley Jameson. 'Cuz the second I can stand, I'm coming for you."

"Good, I'll be waitin'. Oh, you know what?" She tried to kick me again, but I blocked her. Taking her down to the shingles with me.

"Didn't see that coming, did you?"

She shook off the haze, spewing, "I hate you, Jackson Pierce."

I didn't waver in replying, "Not as much as I hate you."

Meaning every last word...

Or so, I thought.

Chapter Sixteen

Jackson

Then: Almost thirteen years old

Twenty-six weeks.
A hundred and eighty-two days.
Four thousand, three hundred and eighty hours.
Six months since my mom left us for Heaven.
In the wake of her death, our lives had changed in such drastic ways. Nothing was familiar anymore, not one damn thing. Our father was never around, drowning himself in work, leaving little time for anything else. Especially his kids. I couldn't remember the last time I saw him walk through the front door, because he never came home.

Whatever was left of Aiden Pierce, our once family-dedicated dad, lived and breathed that fuckin' hospital.

He didn't give a shit about us anymore.

Not even the baby girl he'd always wanted.

It didn't help that Noah and Skyler stepped in for him, taking care of *his* responsibilities. Explaining to us they'd promised our mom they'd be here for our family, or what was left of it anyway, in any way, shape, or form. It was like our mother already knew what was going to happen after she was no longer with us.

Fully aware our father would leave right along with her the day she took her last breath.

He did.

I didn't know what was worse, assuming we were so easily forgettable or thinking he just couldn't be near us at all. I always knew my mother was his everything, but I thought and believed we were a part of that too.

Journey didn't even know his touch, his love, his devotion to give us everything. Never expecting anything in return. She had no idea who he was, which was sad in itself. He had yet to hold his own flesh and blood, his only daughter, in his arms. My baby sister lost both her parents all in the same day, and I hated that for her.

For my brother.

For me.

Jagger was becoming more reclusive than he normally was. He'd always been the quiet one, although now, you wouldn't know he was around at all.

I spent more and more time with Journey, wanting to feel close to my mom. She was the spitting image of her with her bright blue eyes, button nose, and wavy brown baby hair. I'd sit with her in the rocking chair in the nursery and thank God everyday she was in our lives to begin with. Having a piece of our mother left behind helped take away the pain, the loss, the loneliness. That not only lived in our hearts, but in our home, which used to be filled with so much love and happiness.

Now, it was filled with nothing but emptiness and loss.

Skylar pretty much lived at our house day in and day out, fulfilling the role of our parent as best she could with having her own life and kids to take care of.

On top of that, she was expecting again. It didn't surprise anyone when they announced it a few months ago. Noah couldn't keep his hands off her.

It was only a matter of time until she could no longer meet the demands we needed, due to having a newborn of her own.

I was terrified of what would happen when that time came...

Would social services get involved? Would they take us away? Split us up? Would we be following in the same footsteps of our parents and be raised in the system too?

The questions were relentless.

If social services did fuck with us, I wouldn't think twice about running away with them. At the end of the day, I'd fight for my siblings. No one would take them away from me.

They were all I had left.

"Bro, are you even listenin'?" Trigger asked, tearing me away from another one of my biggest fears.

"Mmm hmm…" I mumbled, walking beside him toward the bus after school.

"I was just sayin' Friday's game we sho—"

"The fuck?" I interrupted, taking in the scene unfolding in front of us. "This asshole again?"

"What?" he muttered, confused.

I nodded to the shit show that had captured half of our school's attention. With Harley Jameson being front and center of it all.

Cash was leaning against the picnic table, strumming his guitar in that pansy-ass, bluesy beat she claimed to love. His head moving side-to-side with his foot bouncing up and down to the tune he was playing.

Boy toy was singing a song.

Not just any song…

Her song.

He'd been singing and playing it for the Gremlin since he'd picked up a guitar, and there she was dancing around in sync with his music. Putting on a show for everyone to see, lost in their own stupid little world together. Baby girl loved the attention, eating up every second of it. Swaying her head like his, closing her eyes while she rocked her hips back and forth.

Being one with the rhythm.

My temper was looming as the bluesy beat went da na na na na na, and then he sang, "There was a girl…"

Da na na na na na.

"And her name was Harley."

Da na na na na na.

"She was the coolest girl."

Da na na na na na.

"In all of the town."

Da na na na na na.

"With her bright blue eyes."

Da na na na na na.

"And snarky fuckin' mouth."

Da na na na na na.

"She was my girl."

Da na na na na na.

"No matter what."

Da na na na na na.

"She'd always be…"

113

Da na na na na na.

"My very best friend."

Da na na na na na.

"Now, forever, then."

Da na na na na na.

It was like we were all outsiders looking in on their tight ass bond.

"Who does he think he is, putting on a show? Thinking he's going to be famous, when we all know he's going to end up performing at the nearest coffee shop for the rest of his pathetic life." My glare shifted to meet Trigger's eyes. "Wanna have some fun?"

"Pierce." He slyly grinned at me. "You know I'm always down for a good time."

"Well..." I cocked my head to the side. "If he wants to be the *Greatest fuckin' Showman*, then let's make it a reality for him today."

Trigger arched an eyebrow, understanding my drift.

"Ten bucks for who can embarrass them the most?"

He nodded, smirking. "I never turn down a bet."

Trigger wasn't lying. That motherfucker never said no to anything the football team or I bet him to do. He was always up for a challenge.

The harder the bet, the more he wanted to show us up.

It *triggered* him. Hence, where he got his nickname.

He didn't waver, beating me to the punch like I knew he would.

Clapping his hands together, he loudly announced, "Step right up, ladies and gents! No need to fear! Come see the dumbass pussy boy and his trained dancin' monkey!"

Cash instantly stopped, making Harley whip around to face Trigger. The crowd fell into a fit of laugher, pointing at the dynamic duo.

Trigger didn't miss a beat, staring only at them as he spun in a slow circle with his arms out in the air. "Only a two-dollar admission to the lamest show on earth!"

Harley bit out, "The only trained animal I see is you, Trigger." Eyeing me, she added, "Jackson, call your lapdog before I give him a taste of what I've been feedin' you all these years."

I fired back, "What's the matter, Gremlin? Can't fight your own battles? Need a real guy to help you out? I don't see your very best friend Cash moving a muscle to defend your honor."

"Fuck off, Pierce! It's you who needs protection from Harley. Better guard those balls, quarterback, we all know who owns 'em."

I growled, stepping toward him but Harley got in my face. "You

114

know better than anyone, Jackson Pierce, *I* can and will fight my own battles. Especially when it comes to *you*. I just can't believe YOU are still tryin' to pick one with me! Cash and I are mindin' our own business, and you two Neanderthals decide to stir shit up. What's wrong with you?"

Everyone went quiet, too busy paying attention to every last word that flew out of our mouths.

"Nothing wrong with me, baby girl. I just know your *daddy* wouldn't appreciate the way you're dancing."

"Ugh Jackson! Why do you gotta be so frustratin'? After everythin' we been through!"

Clenching my jaw, I snarled, "Shut your mouth, Harley."

No one knew what happened between us on the roof. We didn't even talk about it.

In my mind, it never happened.

I didn't give a shit what she assumed in her fairytale-filled little brain. We hated each other.

End. Of. Story.

She met my heated stare, spewing, "Or what?"

I scoffed out a chuckle, I couldn't help it. "You want to play with me?" I held my phone up and threatened, "Don't make me send this video of you dancing like you're working a pole to your daddy."

Her eyes widened. "What? You filmed me?"

"Did I fuckin' stutter, Gremlin?"

She reached for my phone. "Give me that!"

I held it higher. "Oh, I'll give it to you... I'll give it to everybody. How do you feel about becoming an internet sensation?! I wonder how long I can get you grounded for this time." With my finger over the send button, I mocked, "Should we find out?"

"Rudolph, don't you dare!"

I smiled, placing my phone in my front pocket. She wouldn't go in there, not when it was so close to my dick.

"I'll just hang on to the evidence... never know when I might need to use it... guess you'll have to wait and see." Leaning in close to her ear where only she could hear me, I whispered, "And I know you love waiting, Harley. Cause we both know you're just *waiting* for me to suck on your tongue again."

She shoved me as hard as she could, but I barely moved an inch. Laughing in her face instead.

"I hate you so much."

115

"You wish you hated me," I baited, meaning it.

"Why are you such a bully?"

"I'm not."

"Yes, you ar—"

I smacked her ass nice and hard. "Now that's being a bully."

"You fresh assho—"

"Alright, students! Break it up! The buses are here and it's time for you all to go home," a teacher ordered, while I blew a kiss and winked at Harley. Reminding her who was boss.

I owned her.

Now.

Forever.

Mine.

Chapter Seventeen

Jackson

She backed away, glaring at me like a rabid dog.

"What just happened?" Shiloh asked, walking up behind her, grabbing her arm. "I was getting my books out of my locker."

"Nothin'. Let's go," Harley replied to her cousin, quickly turning to walk toward the bus.

"You owe me ten bucks," Trigger celebrated, knocking his elbow into mine. "I kicked your ass."

I handed it over, mouthing off, "Don't go spending it all in one place, ya hear?"

"That's your girls' cousin, right?" he asked about Shiloh.

"Mmm hmm."

"You wish she was your girl," Cash chimed in, catching me off guard.

Pussy boy wanted to go one-on-one with me now.

I crossed my arms over my chest. "If I wanted Harley, I could easily have her. Trust me, she'd forget your name by the time I was done with her."

"You mean like your mom forgot yours."

I jerked back like he had punched me in the face.

"Shit, man." He shook his head. "I didn't mean that."

"Yes, you did. Man up, you fuckin' pussy." With that, I rammed my shoulder into his before confidently striding my way to the bus.

Trying like hell to keep my shit together.

That hurt.

Hurt so bad, I found it hard to breathe.

Bringing back all the times my mom raged, yelling I wasn't her son.

"I don't know you!"

"I'm not your mother!"

"Get out of here!"

"Get away from me!"

"I hate you!"

"Jackson, it's your stop!" the bus driver called out, making me realize I was lost in my own mind the entire ride home.

I nodded, getting off the bus with Jagger by my side.

"You alright?" he questioned, looking worried.

"Yeah. I'm fine."

"You don't look fine."

I snapped, "I said I was fine."

"Whoa." He held his hands up. "I was just asking."

I brushed him off, too pissed to apologize. As soon as we got home, Jagger was the first to walk in, followed by me slamming the door shut. The walls vibrated with the wrath I was feeling deep in my bones.

Livid from the turn of events. These emotions were playing with my head, and they were starting to give me whiplash.

I rushed into the kitchen, roughly throwing my backpack onto the island. Overhearing Journey's wails rumbling out of her full force. Getting louder and louder from her nursery. If she didn't stop soon, she was going to make herself sick.

I grabbed a water bottle from the fridge, taking it down in one long gulp. Dehydrated from the madness running through my veins.

"You mean like your mom forgot yours."

"What's up with you? Coming into the house and slamming the front door like that," Skyler reprimanded, fueling the fire coursing in my blood. "Journey could have been sleeping."

"I'd never hurt my baby sister."

"Of course, you wouldn't." She grimaced. "Where is that coming from?"

Jagger intervened. "Jackson's just being a dick."

"Screw you!"

"Jackson! Jagger! What's wrong with you two?"

"Nothing's wrong with me. I'm simply stating the obvious. My brother's being a dick."

"Hey!" she scolded. "Enough of that!"

118

"Wow, Jagger, you actually spoke words today. I'm surprised you still remember how."

"I'm just calling it like I see it, *dick*."

"I'll show you who's a dick." I moved toward him, but Skyler got in between us. Exactly how her niece did with Cash and I at school.

"Jackson, control your temper! I swear you're just like your father."

My mom used to say the same thing to me all the time, and the mere thought further pissed me off.

"Whatever," I muttered under my breath, sliding past her to go to my bedroom. Where I could be alone with the truth Cash threw in my face.

"Jackson! What is up with you?!" Skyler called out behind me down the hallway.

I didn't answer, ignoring her nosey ass.

"Hey! I'm talking to you!"

One foot in front of the other, don't stop. Just go.

"I said, I'm talking to you!"

"Oh my God, Sky! Just back off! We don't want or need you here! Go home and raise your own damn kids!"

"Jackson! Don't you walk away from me! You come back here right now!"

If she wanted a piece of me, then she was about to get it.

"Screw you, Sky!" I spun around. "I'm so sick of your shit! You're just as big of a pain in the ass as your niece! But at least I can make Harley go away! Wish I could say the same for you!"

"Jackson, I get it! You're angry! We're all angry! Do you think this is easy on any of us?"

"You don't know anything! Especially not how I'm feeling!"

It was the truth.

No one knew what I was going through.

Not one damn person.

"Jackson, I'm just trying to help!"

"Nobody wants your help!" I shouted, grinding my teeth. "When are you gonna get that?"

"You need my help, your dad needs—"

"My dad?" I scoffed out with pure disgust you could feel through the walls. "You're seriously going to play that card? Oh, come on, Sky! That's a joke and you know it!"

"That's not fair. Your dad needs you now more than ever, and you being a little shit doesn't help any!"

"Where's my dad, Sky?! Huh? Tell me! Where's the man who needs me? Cuz I haven't seen him in months! Why would he come home when you're always here taking care of his responsibilities? How many times do I have to tell you, you're not my mother?! So just turn your ass around and go home for once! Nobody wants you here!"

Out of nowhere, I heard a voice I didn't recognize, roaring, "Jackson Pierce, you do not talk to her that way!"

Instantly, everyone's heated glares shifted to the woman standing with a peaceful Journey in her arms. Her eyes widened when she realized what she had just done.

Narrowing my eyes at her, I scanned her up and down with a demeaning stare. "Who the hell are you?"

"Jackson," Skyler snarled, bringing my attention back to her. "I'm interviewing her to possibly be your new nanny."

My mouth dropped open. "Are you fuc—"

"Boy, you finish that sentence and I swear I will wash your mouth out with soap. Do you understand me?" the woman warned, interrupting me.

"Oh … this is bulls—"

The expression on the chick's face was enough to render me silent.

I scowled, shaking my head as I backed away. "Whatever." Eyeing only the woman, I assessed her again. Except this time, I really took my time taking her in.

She was young.

Latina.

Pretty.

Closer to my age than my old man's, that was for damn sure.

My friends would like her. A lot.

I cocked an eyebrow with a predatory regard. "At least Mary Poppins is hot. Maybe her ass will make my dad leave the hospital and come home for once."

She jerked back, and Skyler seethed, "Jackson Pierce! You apologize! Right now!"

I rolled my eyes, snidely smiling. "You're the one who hired her, right?" I shrugged. "Should have thought of that before you decided we needed a babysitter. I am a growing boy, after all. So now what? Should we call you Mommy?" I asked her.

"Oh my God, Jackson," Skyler bellowed, her face turning bright red from embarrassment.

Mirroring Mary 'fuckin' Poppins.

Before anyone said another word, I angrily turned around and stormed into my bedroom. Slamming the door so hard behind me, it rattled the walls.

I waited, listening to them intently at the door.

Skyler sighed deeply with humiliation I could feel through the drywall.

"Wow... that is not how I thought this would go down," she expressed. "I'm so sorry, Camila."

Camila?

"I completely understand if you no longer want the position. I truly apologize for wasting your time." I quickly heard Skyler's footsteps. "I'll see you out." Seconds later, she stopped. "I have to ask. That song... the song you were singing to Journey. Why that song?"

I didn't have to wonder long what Skyler meant because Mary Poppins answered, "The *Annie* song?"

The Annie song? The one that made Skyler's career?

"Yeah," Skyler agreed. "Out of all the songs you could sing to her, why that one?"

She was singing to Journey? Is that why she was so quiet?

Over the last month, Journey would fall into a fit of fury only I could stop. I understood her, feeling the same way she was.

I wanted my mom and dad too.

"Oh..." Mary Poppins coaxed. "Um... I used to sing it to my siblings all the time. They loved it. I mean, my sisters must have watched the original movie a thousand times."

"You never saw the remake?"

"No. Why?"

"You really don't know who I am, do you, Camila?"

My eyebrows lowered.

She didn't know who Skyler was?

Everyone knew who Skyler Bell was. We couldn't walk into a gas station without someone asking for a picture or autograph. She used to be the biggest celebrity in the world. Until she married Noah and became Skyler Jameson.

"I'm sorry, I don't know—"

"Please don't apologize," Skyler interrupted her. "When I first promised Bailey I'd be here for her family, I was terrified I wouldn't find the right woman to help me take this on. I had this nagging fear the women I interviewed would be here for the wrong reasons. For who I

121

am and not for the kids. I didn't want to mess it up, you know?"

She did? I didn't know that.

"Bailey's my best friend."

She was your best friend, she died.

This was one of the hardest parts about my mother's death. No one talked about it. It was as if we were waiting for her to come back home, walk through the front door at any moment, knowing in our hearts it would never happen.

She was gone, and nothing or no one could bring her back.

Yet still, we all couldn't speak about it.

All aware it didn't end with her. It had only just started. Jagger, Journey, and I carried her blood, her DNA. We all had the same chance to lose our minds. It was easier to pretend, but inside...

I was ticking away.

Tick...

Tick...

Tick...

When would I go boom?

Tearing my train of thought back to them, Skyler continued on, "She's the older sister I always wanted. When we first met, she didn't know who I was either, and because of that, I loved her instantly. To go from my world, to one where no one knows who I am, was something I prayed for every night. I used to be a celebrity, an actress, and singer. It was a hard life, and if you Googled my name you'd know why. So, to finally find that in her... well, it meant... everything. I guess I'm just trying to say that," she breathed out. "I don't know what I'm trying to say."

Skyler definitely went through some shit, falling down the Hollywood rabbit hole.

Mary Poppins didn't hesitate in saying, "Like me being here is meant to be."

"Yeah, but that's crazy, right?"

"No. I don't think that's crazy at all."

I resisted the urge of screaming, *"It is fuckin' crazy! Nobody wants you here!"*

Without thinking twice about it, Mary Poppins followed it up with, "When can I start?"

If she thinks this is where she was meant to be, then I'd just have to prove...

How wrong she was.

Chapter Eighteen

Jackson

The next morning, I left my house bright and early, walking my ass to school instead of waiting on the bus. Wanting to avoid Skyler and my newest pain in the ass.

Our nanny.

School was the same shit on a different day. I ignored Harley and her Scooby Doo gang all day, not even looking her way, paying her no mind which in turn pissed her off.

Good.

I had enough bullshit in my life at the moment. I didn't need The Gremlin's crap too.

"Harley's cousin," Trigger stirred. "What's her story?"

"Who cares?"

"I do."

"Since when?" I grilled, completely taken back while we ran our drills during football practice.

"She's cute."

"She's alright."

"She's fuckin' smart too. All her classes are advanced."

"Jesus, man, you looked into her classes? Stalk much?"

"Fuck you," he laughed. "I like a challenge."

"Good luck barking up that tree. She's a prude."

"Even better."

"Trigger, don't—"

"Oh, come on, don't give me that shit. After everythin' you put prissy pants Harley through."

"It's different."

"How?"

"It just is."

"Again, how?"

"She belongs to me."

"And I'm the stalker?"

"You wouldn't get it."

"Explain it to me."

"The hell, man? You want to hold hands too? When did you grow a fruity tooty?"

"What the fuck is a fruity tooty?"

I chuckled, remembering the expression on Harley's face the first time I heard her say it to Cash in the shed at the clubhouse years ago.

"When did you grow a pussy? Better?"

"Much. And from what I hear, my cock is much bigger than yours."

"You wish, bitch."

"Speakin' about cocks, when are you gonna let Kate suck yours?"

"When I know I won't need a shot for a STD after."

"You can't get herpes from a blowjob. Wait. Can you get herpes from a blowie?"

My eyes widened. "Trigger, keep your dick in your pants for once."

"But my cock is amazin', it should be shared wit' the cheerleadin' squad. Oh, wait... it has been."

I laughed, shaking my head.

"Don't be a hater. They want ya just the same."

"I'm good."

He threw my words back at me, "The hell, man? You want to hold hands now? When did *you* grow a *fruity tooty*?"

"I don't have time for that shit."

"Then ya make time."

"Trigger—"

"I'm serious, bro. Your balls are gonna fall off. I'm settin' somethin' up for this weekend. Me, you, Kate, and Valerie, it's for your own good."

Before I could tell him no, Harley caught my eye. She was walking with Cash.

What were they still doing here?

125

Trigger followed my gaze. "I mean, unless it's Harley you want."

"Screw her."

"That could be arranged, but you should crawl before you run. Practice makes perfect, football star."

"I don't think that's the expression."

"Alright, how 'bout this? Get your dick sucked before ya fuck Harley's face. Better?"

"Don't talk about her that way."

He jerked back, grinning like the fool he was. "Jackson loves Harley," he sang, smiling from ear to ear.

"Fuck off."

"Oh, this is perfect. We could double date. Just needta put in a good word wit' Shiloh for me. I know! Tell her 'bout my huge dick."

"I'll get right on that."

"Thanks, bro." He patted my back. "Kate!" he shouted across the field to the cheerleading squad running around the track.

"Trigger—"

"I got this. You'll thank me later."

"You assho—"

And he was gone, running his ass toward her.

I sighed, shaking my head again. Observing as Harley's eyes trailed Trigger.

Did she know what he was doing? For me?

"Pierce!" Coach hollered, making her eyes connect with mine. "You're up!"

I nodded, slowly backing away.

"Pierce, move your feet!"

There was something in her expression that caused me to linger for a second.

Was she jealous?

"Pierce, NOW!"

I called out, "I'm coming!"

I spent the rest of practice not giving her another thought. Focusing on bigger and better things.

Never did I imagine what I would be walking into when Jagger and I got home.

"Alright, Miss Thang," Mary Poppins alerted as soon as I opened the garage door.

Bringing my finger up to my lips, I silenced Jagger. Nodding to the living room where her voice was coming from.

126

"How about we kick up the mood around here?"

"Gah!" Journey babbled.

"My thoughts exactly," she replied.

We hid behind the wall where we couldn't be seen, watching as she set Journey in her glider. She grabbed her phone out of the back pocket of her jeans and plugged it into the radio.

After figuring out how to work the thing, she hit play on what I assumed was her playlist. A catchy housebeat blared off the speakers in the open room.

Journey instantly started giggling and jabbering, shaking her body and kicking her legs. My mom loved music, and for most of her pregnancy, my dad played it for her. It always made her come back to us.

"Oh, I see you, gurl! You like to dance, huh?" She grabbed my baby sisters' chubby little arms, clapping her hands together to the beat of the tune. "Like this." Mary Poppins started rocking her hips, left to right, but it wasn't until she twirled around in a body roll that I pulled out my phone.

Turning on the camera.

Journey beamed as I hit record.

I guess I could make my nanny an internet sensation. Already knowing the title of my YouTube video.

Nannies Gone Wild.

"That's the washing machine move. Stick with me, Little Miss, and your milkshake will bring all the boys to the yard."

Journey giggled, throwing her head back.

"This is another one, I call it the booty pop. Ready?"

"Gah!"

It was all the approval she needed to continue dancing for her. The song played on as did her performance.

At one point, she even grabbed the Windex and sprayed it on the windows while shaking her tits.

If Skyler could only see her now…

Journey giggling and having the time of her life was reason enough to keep the nanny dancing for her.

"Alright, now this, baby girl. This is what brings all the boys to my yard. You ready?"

"Gah!"

The beat dropped as fast as did her ass. Getting lower and lower to the ground beneath her. I could see all the views she'd get, and hopefully

127

fired as well.

"Now this is my closing move, Journey. This seals the deal, ya feel me?"

"Bah!"

"You ain't ready! You ready?"

"Bah! Gah! Bah!"

Right then and there, she was about to do something, but when she looked up, she came face to face with us.

"Oh crap." Hauling ass to the radio, she instantly shut it off.

Skyler picked the perfect minute to walk through the front door, the timing couldn't have been better if I'd planned it myself. Her eyes trying to figure out what was going on.

Mary Poppins opened her mouth to explain, but I beat her to the punch, bringing their attention over to me.

With my phone still aimed directly at her, I remarked, "Thanks, Skyler, for hiring us our own private stripper."

Mary Poppins mouth dropped open, noticing the phone in my hand.

She defended herself, "Jackson, that's not what I was doing. I was dancing for Journey and making her laugh."

I snidely grinned and without saying another word, I turned and left. Clicking save on the video, adding to the countless footage I had on my phone.

Jagger followed close behind with his head hanging low, but it was the soft chuckle and smile on his face that had me smiling and chuckling too.

My brother hadn't smiled or laughed in I don't know how long. I hated Mary Poppins, but that didn't change the fact that she at least got my brother to smile and laugh that day.

Even if it was at her expense.

Chapter Nineteen

Jackson

"That's the washing machine move. Stick with me, Little Miss, and your milkshake will bring all the boys to the yard."

It didn't take me long to edit and upload the incriminating video onto YouTube, making sure to keep the best parts. It was a nice distraction from feeling so alone in my own darkness.

The nights were definitely the hardest, lying in bed, staring at the ceiling with nothing but silence surrounding me. My thoughts were unforgiving and endless, making sleep almost impossible most of the time. There wasn't anything to focus on other than my parents not being here for us.

I tossed and turned until I finally passed out from exhaustion. Only to dream about one of the things that haunted me the most. Every night it was the same nightmare, except it wasn't a nightmare at all.

I shook my head, angrily scoffing out, "Fuck this." In two strides, I was walking out of the room, but Dad grabbed my arm stopping me.

"I know you're angry," he voiced, staring into my eyes. "I understand, alright? But you don't want to do this. Trust me, Jackson, if you walk out of here and you don't say goodbye to your mom, it's going to haunt you forever. And I don't want that for you. Please, Son, say goodbye to your mother."

"Don't you get it? She's not here to say goodbye to. There's nothing left of the woman who loved me, raised me, told me she'd always be here for me. She's already gone!" I roared, tearing my arm out of his grasp, nodding over to her bed.

My glare.

My rage.

Stayed consumed on her, wanting to look at her one last time.

"That's not my mom. I don't know who that is."

I gasped, shooting straight up in my bed. My hand holding my heart on my chest, loudly panting. Desperately trying to find my breath.

I couldn't even tell myself it was only a dream…

It wasn't.

It was my reality.

"Jackson," Harley announced, knocking on my door. "You alright?"

Sometimes she'd come with Skyler in the morning, and I hated when she did.

"Get lost!"

"I'm comin' in."

"I said, get lost!"

She didn't listen. She never fuckin' listened.

"Hey." She closed the door, immediately blushing and peering down at the floor. Realizing I was shirtless, wearing only boxer briefs, and still in bed. I'd kicked the sheets off during sleep.

"What, Gremlin? Did you come in here to check out my morning wood?"

"Ewww… gross. No."

"Then what do you want?"

"Ummm…" She played with the seam of her stupid sequined shorts that didn't match her shirt.

"Get dressed in the dark again?"

"*Actually,* this outfit is from this super stylish store online. You wouldn't know cuz you dress like everyone else."

"You mean like a normal person?"

She rolled her eyes. "I didn't come here to talk about my amazin' fashion sense."

"Harley, if you're going to barge into my room uninvited, you need to look at me."

"Fine. Cover your willy first."

"Let me find a big enough blanket."

"Ugh."

"*Actually*" I smiled innocently, grabbing a piece of gum from my nightstand, "hand me the sheet from the floor."

She reached down to grab the cotton fabric, handing it over to me

130

with her eyes still focused down at her feet. As soon as my fingers touched hers, I gripped onto her hand and dragged her toward me.

"Jackson! Don't you dare!"

I laughed, "Like that's gonna stop me." In two seconds flat, I sat her on my lap. With her back facing my front, I bearhugged her from behind and held her in place.

"Jackson! I can feel your willy!"

"Maybe next time you'll think twice before barging into my room."

"You're disgustin'!"

"What's wrong, Gremlin? Never felt anything so big before? If you get tired of my tongue in your mouth, we could use this." I thrusted my hip into her ass.

She gasped loudly.

"Why did you come in here?"

"I can't talk to you when I can feel your balls on my butt, Jackson."

"You hit them all the time with your feet and knees. How's this any different? Tell me what you want, or I'll thrust into your ass again."

"UGH!"

"Shhh… or Skyler will come in here."

"Yeah, girls ain't allowed in your room."

"You're a Gremlin not a girl. Now talk. What do you want?"

She sighed, giving in. "Did ya really record a video of me dancin'?"

"You bet your ass I did."

"Are you gonna send it to my dad?"

"Are you going to be a good little girl?"

"Jackson… you know my daddy would lock me up in my room for the rest of my life if you send him that video."

"More reason to hand it over to him then."

"I'll do whatever ya want for that video."

I jerked back. "What?"

"You heard me."

"Now that's a loaded statement if I ever heard one, Harley Jameson."

"Well, Jackson Pierce, you ain't givin' me much of a choice, are you?"

I turned her around, making her face me. She was now straddling my lap.

"Holy crap! How did you do that so fast?"

"Shhh… you're going to get us in trouble."

"If Skyler comes in here, she's gonna get the wrong idea, and we'll both be grounded for life."

"Then, shut up."

She glared at me.

"So, anything, huh?"

"Yes, but first you have to show me the video, and I havta see you delete it."

"Don't trust me?"

"Never."

"Which video? I got lots."

"What?"

"You heard *me*."

"You have videos of me?"

"Maybe."

"Why?"

"Why not?"

"Not this shit again. Answer my question. Why do ya got videos of me?"

I didn't really know how to answer her, so I simply shrugged.

"That ain't fair."

"Life's not fair."

"Do you like me?"

"I like art."

"What's that supposed to mean?"

"You'll figure it out."

"Figure what out?"

"On second thought," I ignored more of her questions, "I don't want to rush into a decision right now. I want to take my time, weigh my options. You know, make sure I'm going to get something really good out of you."

"You just wanna torture me longer."

I grinned.

"Can you let me go now?"

"I'm barely holding onto you. You could've gotten off my lap already if you wanted to."

"You're holdin' this video over my head. I don't wanna piss you off and you send it."

"You not being on my lap would piss me off?"

"Are you really askin' me that?"

I scoffed out a chuckle.

"Anythin' I don't do when you want me to pisses you off."

"I own you, that's why."

"You wish, dickhead. Oh, and uh..." She smirked in that '*I'm Harley Jameson and I'm about to sass you*' kind of way. Leaning forward, close to my ear, she proved my theory. Stating, "I don't really feel nothin' that big."

"You little shi—"

She jumped off me before the last word left my mouth, darting toward the door and opening it.

"Careful, Rudolph, or Skyler will hear us."

I threw a pillow at her. "Get out."

"Finally." She dodged it. "Something I've been wantin' to do." Spinning on the heels of her Converse sneakers, she turned and left, closing the door behind her.

I fell back into my bed. "Fuckin' Gremlin." Laying there for a few minutes to wrap my head around the rest of the day. Muttering to myself, "Homeroom, PE, Algebra, Science, Computer, football practice."

I started doing this a few years ago. Every morning, I'd go over what my schedule was for the day, wanting to stimulate my mind and memory.

When my mom was first diagnosed, I became obsessed with searching the web to try and find as much information on her disease. Reading several articles that said it was important to consistently get the wheels rolling in your brain. I did this with almost everything, from my schedule, to the names of my friends, to how many steps it took to get to each class at school.

Was it normal?

Probably not, but it'd become my routine.

After I threw on my football jersey and got dressed, I went into the kitchen to grab a strawberry Pop Tart on my way out the garage door.

By the time I got to the bus stop, Gremlin and her Scooby Doo gang were already there. I walked up to Trigger and some other friends from the football team, shooting the shit about nothing while we waited for the bus to take us to school.

"Go talk to Shiloh for me," Trigger exclaimed, nodding over to her.

"You were being serious about her?"

"Do I ever not mean what I say? Especially when it comes to chicks?"

Lucky agreed with me, "Bro, she's not your type."

"I like tastin' all flavors of the rainbow."

"Okay, you're not her type," I added.

"She's never had a guy. How do ya know what her type is?"

"Damn. How much did you ask around about her?"

"I like to know all the facts. Makes it easier to catch my prey."

"Trigger, I don't thi—"

"Jackson!" a familiar and annoying voice hollered, dragging my attention from my friends.

"Ooooohhhh weeee!" they chanted and cheered.

See... I knew my friends would like her.

Mary Poppins was standing several feet away, putting some much-needed distance between us.

She must have seen my YouTube video, and I grinned at the thought. My eyes promptly shifted over to Harley, who was looking back and forth between me and the new nanny.

I winked at the Gremlin before making my way over to Mary Poppins with the swagger of a man. If she wanted to go toe-to-toe with me, then I was going in balls deep.

"Hey, baby," I greeted for all to hear. "You here to dance for me and my friends?"

She didn't hesitate, not once was she going to back down. "Why don't you show them the moves you've been perfecting with Dance Revolution on your Xbox?"

My eyes immediately widened, and I could feel my face turning a bright shade of red.

Someone was snooping...

"Oh, I'm sorry. Was that a secret? Jackson, if you needed dance lessons, you could've just asked me. No need to film me to learn a few moves."

"Shut up," I warned under my breath, standing in front of her.

"But, Jackson? What am I going to do with this new dance footage I have for you?" She held up her phone in the air. "I'm only trying to help you find the rhythm you're obviously lacking based on the level your game is at. Beginners 101—"

I stepped toward her. "I mean it. Shut your mouth, Camila."

"Oh, so you do know my name?" she replied in a much softer tone. "I couldn't tell with how many times you called me Mary Poppins in the comments section."

"What do you want?"

"Take the video down, or I'll out you to your friends with how many dancing games you really do have."

"It's not what you think."

It wasn't.

She had no business going through my things.

"Hey, guys—"

"They were my mom's," I interrupted, rendering her speechless. "I'll take it down, alright? Now, leave."

"Jackson, did you just say they *were* your mom's?"

"I said, *leave*. You don't know shit." I wasn't going to be the one to break the news that the happy little family she saw through the photos on the walls no longer existed.

"I'm just trying to help."

"Then why don't you go shake your ass on a pole where you belong, instead of at my house where nobody wants you," I spoke the truth.

She frowned, unable to form words. Watching me back away with a much different expression on her face than the one she arrived with. Feeling the sense of loss because I'd won this round.

Me: 1

Mary Poppins: 0

Exactly how it was going to continue to stay.

Chapter Twenty

Harley

Dear Jackson "Creeper" Pierce,

It took my mom five hours to get out the gum u stuck in my hair when I was at your house the other day. You're lucky I didn't have to cut it off! Cuz I would have come for your balls!

You're the biggest dick EVER.

I couldn't even tell my mom it was u, so you'd be grounded FOREVER cuz u still have that stupid video! It's been a month, u asshole! Just tell me what u want me to do, cuz I'm over this. I don't care anymore. I'll do whatever u want to stop this frustrating and extremely aggravating control u have over me!!!!

AND YES I'M SCREAMING AT U!

I'm so happy your nanny has stepped in and taken over pranking u. How many girly dance videos do u have, u creeper?! I bought new curtains this wkend, just in case u look into my room when I don't know. The last thing I want is u recording a video of me naked or something.

I. Hate. U.

I just want u to know I laughed my ass off like the rest of the locker room, when I heard about the red Kool-Aid tampons she stuffed in your backpack. U deserve that and more. I can't wait to see what she does to u next.

Not love,
Harley

P.S. Are u dating Kate now? I heard she has the gift that keeps on giving, and I hope u catch it and your willy falls off. Cuz we both know who owns your balls.

Me.

I do.

Jackson

Dear Harley "Peeping Tom" Jameson,

I was just trying to do u another favor. Your frizzy ass hair makes u look like a Poodle. Most of the time, I feel like I should be barking at u. I wish u had to cut your hair cuz maybe u would look better.

Probably not.

And yes, I do have the biggest dick EVER. I knew u noticed.

I haven't figured out what I want u to do yet. There're just way too many choices that will fuck with u. I want to make sure it's nice and hard.

I couldn't even tell u were screaming at me. Your loud ass mouth never shuts up. It's hard to interpret when you're speaking or shouting, so thanks for the heads up.

Don't worry, I'd never creep into your room. I want to keep my eyesight, and if I ever saw u naked, I'd have to tear my own eyes out.

Not that there's anything to see, but u know... That's why I have tons of other dancing girls on my phone...

I hate u way more, Gremlin.

And again, don't u worry, I paid my nanny back. This prank is the best one yet. I'm sure 'Don't Answer' on her phone will appreciate it as much as I do.

With all my hate for u,
Jackson

P.S. Jealous, Harley? Who's the one who holds your freedom in their hands?

Me.

I do.

I stuffed the letter in her locker at the end of the day and went straight home. Keeping my distance from the woman who had become my strongest opponent.
Camila.
Harley was good, but she was better.
Within the last month, our battles had taken a turn for the worst. During her second week at the house, I tricked her. The moment she stepped away from the food she was cooking to tend to my baby sister, I decided to play chef.
Dumping in three different bottles of hot sauce we had in the cabinets. She spent an hour in the bathroom throwing up from her nose and mouth.
The next day, she fed it to me for lunch without me realizing until it was too late. I spent an hour in the bathroom doing the same thing she was the day prior.

138

By the third week, I scribbled all over her notes from her anatomy class. Mary Poppins was going to school to be a nurse.

She failed her quiz the following day, which prompted her most recent attack on me. Planting Kool-Aid soaked tampons in my backpack for all to see in the locker room. I was the laughingstock of the school for the rest of the day.

I played it off like it wasn't a big deal. I was Jackson Pierce, I could make anything look good.

Inside though, I was fuckin' fuming.

I hated her.

She only accepted this position because of Skyler. We were a job to Camila, no matter what she claimed. Telling me she was there for us.

Bullshit.

We were a paycheck.

Nothing more, nothing less.

I spent the entire week thinking of how I would get my revenge. What I would do to her next. Once I saw 'Don't Answer' calling her phone, I knew...

I texted him back pretending to be her, letting him know she wanted the D.

Zero regrets.

Until this very moment.

I'd barely been awake for more than a minute when she took it upon herself to charge into my room.

"What the hell?" I gritted, jumping off my bed in my gym shorts. "You can't just barge into my room without knocking."

"You cannot invade my privacy like that, Jackson!"

"Why not?" I countered with a snide expression. "You do ours."

"I haven't done anything to deserve this level of disrespect from you!"

"You sound really bitchy, Camila. Guess 'Don't Answer' on your phone didn't lay the D down right?"

Her mouth dropped open. "You cannot talk to me like that!"

"Alright," I responded, not caring in the least. "Then leave."

"You'd love that, wouldn't you? For me to just quit."

"Yeah, I would," I replied with no hesitation, walking over to my dresser to grab a shirt.

"And then what, Jackson? You're just going to treat the next nanny the same way? Until what? Your mom comes back? Is that why you can't stand me? Why you want me to quit so badly? Because you think

139

it's going to make your mom come home?"

I stepped up to her, getting right in her face. "Shut your mouth, Mary Poppins. You have no idea what you're talking about."

She still didn't know the truth about our mother, and I didn't care enough about this intruder to tell her what was up. Besides, it was driving her insane not knowing where Mr. and Mrs. Pierce were, busy coming up with all these theories in her mind.

I enjoyed watching it too much.

If she was going to be a pain in my ass, then I was going to return the fuckin' favor.

It was as simple as that.

"You're right, I don't. All I know is, if I had a kid like you, I'd leave too."

I wasn't expecting her to say that, and it caught me off guard. No one had ever spoken to me like that before. For some reason I couldn't describe or justify, it hurt.

Judging by the regret etched into her face, it must have shown in my eyes.

Now, she was the one who crossed the line.

"I didn't mean tha—"

"Get out!"

"Jackson, come on... you know I didn't mean that."

"I don't know shit."

"Exactly! Because you haven't taken the time to actually get to know me. You spend all your time and energy hating someone you won't even give a chance. I'm just trying to help you."

"I don't need your help!"

"Then what, Jackson? You're just going to spend the rest of your life not needing anyone? Is that the way you want to live?"

"I said get out!" I snarled through a clenched jaw. My fists pumping at my sides.

"Or what? Huh? What are you gonna do? I'm not scared of you. If anything, I feel bad for you. You push everyone away. Every single person. Including your own family. One day you're going to need them, and I hope it's not too late. Because regardless of the bullshit you keep putting me through, I'm not going anywhere. I love your baby sister, and if you gave me half the chance, I could be here for you too."

I shook my head in disgust.

Who the hell did she think she was?

She didn't know me...

What I'd been through…

What I continued to go through every damn day.

Losing my mother.

My father.

Possibly my memory.

Fuck her.

I spit fire. "I don't need your pity. So why don't you go sell your spiel to someone who gives a shit about you? Cuz we both know, I sure as hell don't."

She jerked back, not hiding how much that hurt her.

Good. Now we were even.

"I'm sorry your parents aren't around, okay? But it's not my fault. I didn't make them go away, Jackson. I was hired because they're not here. You need to realize that and stop blaming me for things that are out of my control," she advised, taking a deep breath and stepping back toward the door. "Don't ever touch my phone again. Do you understand me?"

I eyed her up and down, cocking my head to the side. Taking in what she just said with as much curiosity as she had about my parents.

"There's a reason his name is under 'Don't Answer' in my phone. You could have…" She sighed, being at her wits end.

"Who is he?" I blurted, surprising myself I actually kind of cared.

"Someone I want nothing to do with."

"Huh," I quickly snapped back. "Well then, maybe now you'll understand. Seeing as I want nothing to do with you. Now get out."

"Alright." She nodded. "I'll get out of your room, but I'm not getting out of your life. I'm here to stay."

"Yeah, for Journey."

"And for *you*." With that, she turned around and left. Closing my door behind her.

I reached for the lock, faltering when I heard my brother on the other side declare, "He wasn't always like this, Camila." Stopping me dead in my tracks.

I swear those were the first words he had ever spoken to her.

"He's mad at my dad. It's not you," he explained, stirring my heart to race. "Journey really loves you. You make her happy. My mom didn't have the chance to do that, and Journey is one of the reasons my dad isn't around."

I grimaced, hating it was the truth.

My baby sister didn't deserve any of what was dealt to her. She didn't ask to be born.

"It doesn't matter what you say or do, my mom isn't coming home. That much I can tell you."

"Is she—"

"I'm sorry Jackson is treating you like this, but Journey isn't the only one who wants you here."

She asked him what I was thinking, "She isn't?"

"No. I want you here too."

He does?

"You do?"

"Yeah."

"Why?"

"Because I think you could fix things."

Why?

How?

"With Jackson?"

"Yeah. And maybe my dad."

"Jagger, what do you—"

I heard his footsteps next and then his door shut, cutting her off.

"It doesn't matter what you say or do, my mom isn't coming home. That much I can tell you."

Those words were like a knife to my heart and yet…

They were the truest words he'd ever spoken.

Chapter Twenty-One

Harley

My daddy was out of town on business which meant Momma was in charge. Meanin' I could go to the party happenin' on Oak Island beach after the football game, Friday night.

I was excited, Daddy didn't allow me to do much. Sayin' he was protectin' me from all the little shits who wanted a piece of his baby girl. Like they wanted a piece of his old lady...

He didn't play around when it came to his family. Raisin' Luke and Owen to be just like him. They were becomin' rabid guard dogs when it came to me as well.

It was actually super annoyin', but I loved my daddy too much to go against his wishes. So, I just didn't tell him everythin'. I wasn't lyin', just withholdin' information he didn't need to know.

Momma always understood me. She was forever on my team. Tellin' me Daddy hadn't changed. He was like that with her when she was my age, and she found it super annoyin' too.

"Trigger keeps starin' over here at you," I told Shiloh, catchin' him lookin' at her for the tenth time that night.

We were dancin' around the firepit on the beach, to Cash's band's live music.

"Well, then let me give him something to look at," she coaxed, spinnin' around.

Instantly, she flipped him the bird.

Makin' me laugh my ass off.

Shiloh was a good ol' girl and just like the boys, she was feisty.

Don't piss her off.

However, she didn't really cuss, got straight A's, and didn't cause problems for her parents.

She was a role model for everyone, includin' me.

All that mattered to her was school and her family. She wanted to follow in her daddy's footsteps to become a lawyer, attendin' Stanford Law like he did too.

But it was more than that, Shiloh was just smart about everythin'. Especially boys. The girl had her head on right and didn't allow bullshit into her life.

She wanted to get married a virgin and everythin'. Only allowin' one lobster to love her for a lifetime.

To say she was picky would be an understatement. She even had a "do's and don't's" list for her future dude to keep her on track and the path she wanted to follow. No one stood a chance to her high standards.

Specifically, the boys at our school.

"I think he likes you."

"He likes the idea of me."

"What do ya mean?"

"I'm way out of his league, Harley, and he knows it. Boys like Trigger only want one thing."

I cocked my head to the side. "Blowies?"

"That and notches on their belts. I'm a challenge to him, and the worst part is, he thinks I'm stupid enough to fall for it. It's offensive."

"Facts. He's cute though."

"He's alright. I'm not into hicks."

"Hey! I'm a hick."

"You're my cousin," she giggled. "And my best friend."

I nodded. "More facts."

She made a heart with her fingers. "Forever and ever, it's me and you, girl."

I made a heart back. "You just spittin' facts now, Shiloh."

We laughed.

"What are they doing over there under the pier anyways?" she asked, shiftin' my gaze to the group of football players, includin' Jackson.

I shrugged. "Bein' shitheads?"

"Do you smell that?"

I took a whiff of the air. "I do now."

"Are they smoking a joint?"

144

My eyes widened, thinkin' of Jackson smokin' pot.

"Yeah, I think they are," she added.

She was right, they were. It was right in his hand.

Before I knew what I was doin', my feet were stompin' their way over to him. Snatchin' the joint from his fingers.

"The fuck, Grem—"

Crudely, I turned and walked straight to the garbage can. Tossin' it where it belonged instead.

By the time I spun back around, Jackson was in my face. Roarin', "What the fuck?"

"Yeah! *What the fuck* is right! What are ya doin'?"

"Mind your own business, Harley."

"No! I will not! Why are you smokin'?"

"Why do you care?"

"Cuz your momma! That's why!"

He immediately gripped onto my arm, draggin' me a little further down the beach where we couldn't be heard. Once we were alone from pryin' eyes, I tore my arm away and gave him a piece of my mind.

"Why do you wanna be a stoner?"

"A stoner? Smokin' pot a few times doesn't make me a stoner. Plus, I got more in my pocket."

"A few times? You've smoked before? Why do you have more of it?"

"How many times do I have to tell you to mind your own fuckin' business, Harley?"

"As many times needed for you not to smoke weed!"

He stepped toward me, loomin'. "Stop fuckin' yelling at me."

"Somebody has to!" I pushed him. "You're better than that, Jackson Pierce! Don't fall for peer pressure like your stupid ass jock friends do!"

"Fuck off!"

I shoved him again.

"Harley…"

"Don't 'Harley' me!"

"You don't know what you're talking about."

"Jackson! Why would you trigger anythin' in your mind that could bring on demen—"

He bit, kickin' up the sand, "Shut your fuckin' mouth, Harley."

"No, I won't! This is stupid! You're bein' stupid! What do you havta prove to anyone? You're the star quarterback, every girl wants ya.

145

You're already a legend in this town cuz of your arm," I reminded, shovin' him as hard as I could that time.

"Stop fuckin' pushing me," he snarled through a clenched jaw.

"No! You deserve it!" I went to shove him again, but he grabbed my arms, turnin' me so my back was to his front.

"Stop being a fuckin' brat, before I really give you something to bitch about!"

I didn't hesitate, liftin' my foot up to kick him in his balls but he blocked it. Holdin' onto me tighter.

"You really need to learn how to control that short Jameson fuse, baby girl." He tugged me closer to his chest. "I wasn't smoking."

"But you had a joint in your hand."

"Did you see me bring it up to my mouth?"

"I don't understand."

"Yeah, you wouldn't. You have both your parents at home. Go home, Harley. You don't belong here. Don't make me text your daddy."

I gasped, "You wouldn't."

"Try me again and watch how fast I send him every last video I have of you."

"Why would you be so evil? What other videos do you have?"

"You'll have to wait and see."

"Jackson, this is bullshit. I'm just tryin' to protect you from doin' somethin' stupid."

"What do you think I'm trying to do?"

I jerked back. I wasn't expectin' him to admit that.

"So, then you do like me?"

"Go. Home. Now." With that he let me go, turned and walked back toward his friends.

"I hate you!" I spewed to his back, watchin' him walk away.

Thinkin' to myself, I couldn't get the words out of my mouth for what I was truly feelin'.

"You have me, Jackson. You're not alone. Cuz you got me."
Sincerely meanin' it...

With each part of my confused, torn heart.

Jackson

I went home shortly after Harley left, wanting to put my plan into action.

Harley didn't have a fuckin' clue, and I wasn't going to allow her temper tantrum to deter me from what I honestly thought would work.

Leaving my jeans where Mary Poppins could find them, I went about the rest of my weekend.

Come Monday afternoon, I strode into my bedroom after school, knowing it was exactly where I'd find our nanny waiting for me.

With a stunned gaze, I played dumb. My eyes roaming from her concerned expression to the bag of weed securely in her grasp.

Hook, line, and sinker...

I grinned. "I didn't know Mary Poppins got high. Is that why she's always so happy?"

"Very funny, Jackson. We both know this isn't mine."

"Are you trying to say it's mine?"

"Who's else would it be? It was in your jeans."

"It's not mine, and I have no idea how it got in there," I lied, egging her on.

"Oh, so it just magically grew legs and jumped in your pocket without your knowledge? Just happened to show up, while I placed them in the dryer to de-wrinkle your clothes? Try again."

Eyeing her skeptically, I threw my backpack on my bed. Witnessing her have a meltdown exactly how Harley had.

"What exactly are you trying to do here? Get me fired? Huh? That's quite the stunt to pull on me, even for you. Skyler could have me arrested! No more nursing school, no more future, no more nanny for you! No more nothing thanks to you. I'm already missing so many classes because I'm here caring for you, instead of showing up for school!"

Offended, I put my hands up in the air. "Hey! I didn't know you were going to dry my jeans. That's on you."

I didn't.

I thought she'd find it before she threw them in the laundry.

"So, you did know the bag was in your jeans?"

Rolling my eyes, I scoffed out, "No. I didn't."

"Then what? Huh? Explain to me what's going on here, before I explain to Skyler what I think is going on instead."

I arched an eyebrow, unfazed.

Finally. We were getting somewhere.

Shrugging, I simply replied, "Then here's your chance to get back at me, Camila. Go tattle, I don't give a shit. Skyler's not my mother and neither are you."

"So, you are smoking weed?"

"Why does it matter to you if I am?"

"You have your whole life ahead of you. You shouldn't be smoking weed, that's why."

"And why is that, Mary Poppins? You're telling me you've never tried it?"

"Nice try. This isn't about me. This is about you."

"Actually, this is about both of us. You brought this on yourself. Stay out of my business and we won't have any problems. Yeah?"

"You know what? You're right about one thing, I'm not your mother, nor do I want to be. Why is it so hard for you to see that? The stunt you pulled today crossed the line, Jackson! This is not okay! You know Journey is with me all the time, and the house reeked of weed because of your ploy to get me fired! Thank God I found a surgical mask to put on her, or else I would have been beyond screwed! You put your baby sister's health in danger!"

"Oh bullshit, you're just being dramatic. There was barely any weed. She was fine."

I'd never do anything to hurt Journey. I thought she'd find it before her dumbass put it in the laundry.

Some housekeeper she was.

"How would you know? Are you in medical school? Do you have a degree in—"

"Camila!" I shouted over her bullshit rambling.

This wasn't about her.

It had nothing to do with her.

She was my means to an end.

"What do you want from me? If you're looking for an apology, you're shit out of luck, cuz you're not getting one."

She stepped up in my face. "Do you have any idea how hard I've worked to get to this point in my life? I didn't grow up like you with your million-dollar house, name brand clothes, and overly-priced education you take for granted." She pointed to herself, standing her ground.

One thing I knew for sure, she wasn't leaving my room until she got her opinion across.

She was going to put me in my place, regardless of the consequences.

"I grew up poor with parents who struggled to put food on the table for all of their kids, but who still provided the best they could under the circumstances. I grew up with hand-me-downs, shopped at thrift stores, bought secondhand everything, just so I could have shoes to wear, a book to read, a calculator to do my math homework with. I didn't grow up with a silver spoon in my mouth like you did! But I'll tell you one thing, Jackson, if I had, you bet your ass I would've appreciated it and not have been a spoiled little shit like you who doesn't know the meaning of the word grateful."

My eyes glazed over. It was quick, but she saw it.

Don't fall for it, Jackson... Stay strong.

"It's not my fault your parents didn't know when to stop having kids."

Her mouth dropped open. "Wow. There is no getting through to you, is there?"

"And yet, here you are, still trying."

She shook her head disappointed, stepping away from me. "I have nothing left to say to you."

"Great, cuz I don't want to hear anymore. Tell Skyler whatever you want, maybe it will make my dad come home for once."

Shit.

Mary Poppins was smart. It wouldn't take her long to put two and two together.

She cocked her head to the side with the realization of what my plan was, slapping her in the face.

Fast and hard.

"This wasn't about me at all, was it?"

"Get out of my room, Camila."

"You want me to rat you out, don't you?"

"I'm not going to say it again," I warned, my temper threatening loud and destructive.

"Jackson, acting out isn't going to bring him hom—"

I got right in her face. "Get out!"

Her feet stumbled as I backed her out of my room, forcing her into the hallway before I slammed the door in her face.

"Jackson!" She banged on the door. "You can't do this! You can't just shut me out like this!"

"I just did!"

"Come on! Give me a chance! All I'm asking for is a chance!"

To both of our disbelief, I actually opened it. Getting right in her face again. "What else do I have to do to—"

"What's going on here?" Skyler announced, breaking up our argument. Catching us both by surprise.

Mary Poppins turned to face her, still feeling my heated stare as she shoved the bag of weed in her back pocket.

Still unsure of what to do.

I watched her every move, just waiting for the other shoe to drop. *Come on... just tell her already.*

"Yeah, Camila, what's going on here?" I baited, wanting to move this along.

"I- I- I- I mean... we were just..."

There was only one way I imagined this would go down. Never in a million years did I think she would be this perceptive.

Never in a million years did I think... she would care.

The more she thought about it, the more she realized who I was and what I stood for. Football was my life, and I wouldn't risk that for anything. It was the only thing I was truly passionate about in life, other than making her and Harley's existence a living, breathing hell.

I wanted my dad home, even if it meant I had to pay the price to make it happen.

Her heart hurt more for me in that moment than it did over the last two months she'd been working for us. It didn't matter how many times I pushed her away, she got right up to go another round with me again.

Mary Poppins opened her mouth to say something but quickly shut it, looking over at me instead. We weren't more than a foot apart, but it felt like miles of distance were placed between us.

Physically and mentally.

The confusion on my face was evident. There was no hiding it, because the truth was, Camila confused me.

As the weeks continued to go by, she started getting in a little. Inch by inch, my guard began to come down toward her.

Don't get me wrong, I still hated her. Though that powerful emotion was geared due to the fact my father was never home. She stepped in, taking his place like Skyler did.

He was never going to come home if there was somebody here.

Why?

He didn't have to.

Did he even love us anymore? Were we even a thought?

Time stood still in that instance, the truth consuming both of us.

She was the first to break our middle ground. Locking eyes with Skyler, she muttered, "Jackson and I were just arguing about his laundry habits."

I stiffened beside her.

"Jackson knows how to do laundry?"

"Or lack thereof," she added, smiling over at me.

I narrowed my eyes at her, more confused than ever before.

She had the chance to rat me out. Get back at me for all the shit I'd put her through, even the playing field once and for all.

She didn't.

She took my side, being there for me.

Making me realize right then and there…

I was just as lost.

As my father was.

Chapter Twenty-Two

Jackson

Then: Thirteen years old

They say everything needs to come to a head.

As the days continued on with no sign of our father, the further my resentment grew to a point of no return.

Another month had flown by and still nothing.

In spite of that, my dynamic with Camila had changed in ways I never expected. Our pranks developed into less hostile territory. We weren't trying to take each other out like we were before. Now they were merely our source of entertainment.

But I was still Jackson Pierce, and I still always won. At everything. Even our nicer pranks.

Jagger and I walked into the house after school one afternoon, suddenly hearing Mary Poppins lose her shit on Journey's stuffed animal in the living room.

Screaming, "Can you hear me? I'm going to find you! And then we're really going to have words!"

"You know that's a stuffed animal, right?" I questioned, looking at her like she'd lost her mind.

She jumped as soon as she heard my voice, whipping around to face me. She yelled, "No! It's your dad!"

My father's absence was affecting everyone in the house.

"Since when did my dad become a bunny's ass?"

"He's in here! I know it!"

I tilted my head to the side, narrowing my eyes at her. "Mary Poppins, Journey is watching you lose your mind on one of her favorite stuffed animals. So, before you traumatize her any more than you already have, put it down and step away from the bunny."

She scowled, stepping toward me, shoving what was left of the stuffed animal into my chest. "Fine. Then I'm going to find the man that's inside the bunny."

"This isn't *Toy Story*, Camila. There's no one inside of it."

"You'll see," she cryptically coaxed, spinning her way toward the garage door.

"Where are you going?!"

"I just told you!"

She sidestepped Jagger, who was standing in the kitchen with a huge grin on his face, as if he knew exactly what she was talking about.

What the hell was going on?

"What about Journey?" I called out after her.

"You can watch her!"

"What? I've never watched her before! You can't just leave her with me! It's not my job to watch her, it's yours!"

"You can handle it for an hour! Just hold her, feed her, change her diaper! You've seen me do it hundreds of times!"

"Mary Poppins, what the fu—"

"Finish that sentence, and I'll wash your mouth out with soap when I get back!" She slammed the door behind her, and there we were left with my baby sister alone for the first time.

"What do we do with her?" Jagger asked, standing next to me. Shaking his head.

"Uh... she seems alright down there."

"For now."

Journey was sitting on her old Ninja Turtle blanket on the floor, gazing at us with an expression like *don't fuck this up or I'll shit on you.*

I slapped Jagger's chest. "Tag, you're it."

"What? Camila said you were responsible for her. Not me. Plus, I think she's dropping a bomb right now."

"Uh... I don't think so."

"She has her poop face going."

"Journey, do you hear what he's saying about you? Tell him you're just flushed cuz Mary Poppins killed your bunny."

"Gah!"

"See." I slapped him again. "She's just chilling."

"Nope. I think she's pushing a turd out." He picked her up, holding her in between us. "Check her."

What other choice did I have, her diapered ass was in my face. "Fine." I pulled her shorts and diaper away from her butt. "Oh my God, Journey! What is she feeding you?"

She fell into a fit of giggles, kicking her legs. Causing the massive explosion in her diaper to get further all up in there.

"What do we do?"

"We're gonna have to change her."

"How?"

"I don't know the rules." I shrugged. "I guess we'll hose her down."

"In the sink or the tub?"

"Sink. She's too small for the tub."

"Good call."

Journey chose that moment to let out the loudest fart, making me and Jagger laugh our asses off.

"You're supposed to be a lady," I said to her, kissing the top of her head.

"She must take after you."

I shrugged again, nodding toward the kitchen. "Let's go before it starts running down her legs."

We gagged the entire time we took her clothes off, resisting the urge to throw up.

"Aim her ass toward the sink, Jagger! The sink! Not my face! Can't you see I'm dying here, man?"

"Excuse me! I'm the one holding her!"

"She's got a hanger, bro! There's a hanger, and I can't get it to come off!"

"Bah! Gah! Mah!" she fumed with fury.

"It's not you, Journey, it's your butt," I reassured her. "That's not normal."

I turned on the sink, testing out the water until it was warm enough to use the sprayer.

I was about to go to town on rinsing her swamp butt down, but Harley intervened, "Holy crap!" she breathed out, walking into the kitchen from the front door. "What are you doing to her?"

"Oh! Perfect timing!" With a big huge smile on my face, I didn't think twice about it. I grabbed Journey out of Jagger's hands, and in three long strides, I was cleaning her dirty ass onto Harley's bright pink shirt.

"Jackson!"

Moving Journey side to side and up and down against the fabric, I made sure the poop chunks were now on Harley's chest.

"There we go." I brought her back to me. "Now we can hose you down."

Harley's mouth dropped open and I grinned. "Thanks for the help."

"Aunt Skyler!" she yelled bloody murder, hauling ass to the bathroom to try and salvage what was left of her horrible shirt.

"What?" I called out after her. "I said thank you!"

Skyler rushed into the kitchen, her eyes darting from us to Journey. "Jackson, what is going on? Where is Camila?"

"She left."

"She left?!"

"Yeah… uh…" I thought quick on my feet, coming up with a reason on why she wasn't here so she wouldn't get in trouble.

She was doing us a solid and going to yell at our father for us, the least I could do was return the favor.

"She umm… had to take her mom to the ER," I lied, covering for her. "She fell down the stairs."

By the look on Skyler's face, she was as shocked as I was, but for a completely different reason.

"She didn't call me."

"Oh, it's cuz I told her not to. I told her I'd tell you."

"Bah!" Journey exclaimed, bringing everyone's attention back to her and her rank ass.

"Come here, baby," Skyler soothed, taking her out of my hands to walk back toward her nursery. "What were your brothers doing to you?"

"Dah, bah, mah!"

I swear my baby sister was a genius. She had to be… she was related to me.

I turned to follow her, but right when I spun around, I was smacked in the face with what I'd least expect.

Harley's shirt.

That still had poop on it.

"Oh, Gremlin… you better fuckin' run."

"I win, always, dickwad." She laughed and took off running.

For the next hour, I was in the shower burning off my skin.

Fuckin' Gremlin.

Skyler spent the night in the guest bedroom, but I was the one who got up with Journey the next morning. Wanting a few minutes alone with her before I went to school.

I was feeling the loss of my mom hard that day.

It was Noah and Skyler's anniversary, and he'd planned a surprise party for her that evening. My mom would have loved planning alongside Noah. It was her favorite type of celebration. She used to go all out for my dad and her's as well.

When Mary Poppins walked into Journey's nursery, she quickly smiled. Watching as I held my baby sister in my arms, rocking her in her chair. This was the first time she'd ever seen me hold her, let alone look down at her with so much tender love and care.

Journey was pulling at my shirt, holding onto it so tight. She didn't want to let go and neither did I.

"You're a natural, Jackson. You're going to make a great daddy one day."

My eyes flew up to hers. "I don't want kids."

"You say that now, but you're so young. You have a full life ahead of you."

I shook my head, snapping in a harsh tone, "I wouldn't talk about things you don't know, Camila."

Her hands surrendered in the air. Addressing the elephant in the room instead, "Thank you for covering for me yesterday. I really appreciate it. You didn't have to do that for me."

Skyler must have told her what I said.

"I didn't do it for you, Mary Poppins, I did it for Journey."

She nodded. "Well, maybe you also did it because you're starting to accept me?" Rocking on the heels of her feet, she added, "You know, maybe even like me? A little, not a lot. Definitely more than you like Harley," she teased, hoping it would tear down some of my walls. Even if it was only for a second.

"You're right," I agreed. "I hate Harley."

She arched an eyebrow. "Do you though?"

"What are you trying to say, Camila?"

"Nothing, just an observation."

"Ah, so the same girly bs she tells me all the time."

"Which is?"

"I'm mean to her cuz I like her."

She shrugged, smirking. "Do you?"

"Fuc—"

She glared at me.

156

"F-u-c-k no."

She laughed, unable to help it. My smartass mouth always had that effect on people.

"You girls watch way too many Disney movies."

"Says the guy who has a few in his room."

It was my turn to glare at her.

Once again, she put her hands up in the air in a surrendering gesture. "What? I didn't put them there."

"Neither did I."

She didn't have to ask to know what I was implying.

"I can move them if you want."

My gaze narrowed in on her, searching for something in her expression before snipping, "Yeah, whatever. Did you find my dad?" I grilled, changing the subject to another discussion I did want to have.

"Kind of."

"Was he working?"

"You could say that."

"His precious hospital is all that matters to him anymore."

"I don't think that's true at all."

"How do you know? Did you talk to him?" I questioned with hopefulness in my voice.

"I could just tell."

"How?"

"I could see it in his eyes. He misses you as much as you miss him."

I jerked back. "I don't miss him."

"Jackson…"

"I don't. I don't need him. To hell with him." There was so much pain in my words, in my tone, in my demeanor when it came to the man who'd given me life.

There was no hiding it anymore.

I wanted nothing more than the chance to go off on him.

"You don't mean that. You're just angry. Trust me, I know what that feels like."

"You think you know everything, don't you, Mary Poppins?"

"I know I've become your punching bag, and I don't care what you tell yourself, I know you don't hate me. But if it makes you feel better to take stabs at me, then so be it. Hit me again, Jackson, because maybe there'll come a day when you can see me as your friend and not your enemy. I'm actually a pretty cool person. If you gave me half a chance, you'd see I'm not a threat to you. To anyone for that matter. I'm not here to replace anybody. I just want to help you."

"And then what? When you're done helping, you what? Just leave us behind?"

"Is that what you want?"

"No."

She smiled, thinking she got through to me.

She didn't.

Not even for a second.

I'd already lost both my parents. I wasn't going to let anyone in my life that I could lose all over again.

It hurt too damn much.

Hastily, I stood. Handing my baby sister over to her.

"Journey wouldn't like that," I declared the truth. "Cuz let's face it, Camila, we both know she's the only one who wants you here."

She grimaced, and for the first time, I felt regret pull at my eyes.

"Did that make you feel better? Because the expression on your face says otherwise."

"Everyone leaves, that's just life."

Her eyes watered, only fueling my anger.

The last thing I wanted was for anyone to feel bad for me. Take pity on me.

Fuck that.

"I'm sorry, Jackson, I hate that you feel that way. I wish there was something I could—"

"What did he say? I want to know what my father said to you."

"That he loves you very much."

I couldn't tell if she was lying or not, but my sister and I hung on to her every word. As if Journey could understand and needed to hear it as much as I did.

Her stare moved all around the nursery until it landed on Journey's bookshelf in the corner of the room.

"Your dad is hurting, and he doesn't want you to see how bad."

"He is?"

"Yes. He broke down."

"In front of you?"

"Mmm hmm."

"After he said he was hurting?"

"Sort of."

"So, my father who'd just met you for the first time, willingly told you all this?"

"Mmm hmm."

"Why do I feel like you're lying?"

Our eyes connected.

"Why would I lie?"

"You tell me."

"I am telling you. Why is it so hard for you to believe that your father loves you?"

"I don't know, Mary Poppins, maybe cuz I haven't seen him since my mom—"

"There you are," Skyler interrupted. "Jackson, you're going to be late for school. You gotta go."

I backed away, nodding. Grabbing my backpack off the floor, I walked out of the room, taking the truth of where my mother was…

With me.

Chapter Twenty-Three

Harley

Then: Twelve years old

"Baby girl, you look beautiful," Daddy complimented me when I strolled into the livin' room. All dolled up for the surprise anniversary party we were attendin'. He was standin' in the entryway with his hands in his pockets, wearin' a black suit, lookin' all handsome.

I twirled around in a circle for him, loving the feelin' of my dress puffin' out at the bottom. "Thanks, Daddy. It's new."

I was beyond excited for the evenin' ahead. Momma and Aunt Lily took Shiloh and me shoppin' for the occasion, spoilin' us like the princesses we were. We spent the whole day together, doin' girly things like gettin' our nails and hair done, talkin' about all the latest drama, includin' how much Trigger was botherin' Shiloh these last few weeks.

With his heated looks and flirty smiles and cocky attitude.

Gossipin' about Jackson Pierce and his wicked ways, too.

It took five different stores for me to find "the dress", the one that fit not only my style, but my figure as well. I picked out a knee-length, light blue strapless dress with matchin' strappy heeled sandals that I never wanted to take off.

Of course, I added my own spin to the flowy material, sewin' a few bows and sparkles on to make it pop and stand out. I hated blendin' in with everyone else. I had my own sense of style, and I didn't keep up with trends.

I was a fashionista through and through, and it only got worse the older I became. One day, I'd have my own online store called *Harley's Closet. Dare to be Different.*

I already knew my color scheme and logo for my social media and website. It would be a photo of me and my future furry best friend. I wanted a Wheaten Terrier, but I refused to buy one. I'd have to wait until a similar breed showed up at the shelter I still volunteered at.

Always rescue first.

"Wow, Harley. You're gettin' so big. Where did my baby girl go?"

My smile lit up my entire face. "I'll always be your baby girl, Daddy."

"I'm gonna hold you to that, sweetheart."

This was the first time he was seein' my dress, and to be honest, I was a little worried he'd think it was too revealin'.

It wasn't.

This was the man who thought my knee-length shorts and skirts were always too revealin'. I assumed Momma was behind his change of heart. She knew how excited I was to be wearin' somethin' more young adult and not childish. I was growin' up, and he needed to accept that.

"You look just like your momma did at your age."

I noddin', agreein' with him. I loved nothin' more than when he'd say those words to me. My momma was the most beautiful woman I'd ever seen. She was breathtakingly stunnin', and I always wished I'd find a man who'd look at me the way my daddy looked at her.

As if she was the only thing that ever mattered in his whole world.

"How are you gettin' so big?"

"That's what happens when you feed me, silly."

He laughed, pullin' me into a hug.

I gazed up at him, settin' my chin on his chest. "Daddy, do you think I'll ever find a boy who loves me like you love Momma?"

"Not before I put him to ground, baby."

"Creed!" Momma shouted, steppin' into the livin' room. "You're horrible. Stop teasing her."

"Who's teasin'?"

I laughed, shakin' my head. Daddy said what he meant and meant what he said.

Always.

This wasn't a shock to me by any means, knowin' all along I'd have to find a guy who'd have to make my father fall for him as well. It'd be the only way I'd ever get to have my own lobster.

With Daddy's approval.

Or else, he really would put him to ground.

No doubt about that.

I hugged him one last time and let him go, fully aware he couldn't wait to hug his wife. Swiftly, he made his way over to her, drawin' her toward him.

"You look good enough to eat, Pippin." He leaned forward, whisperin' in her ear.

I smirked, knowin' he was sayin' somethin' really dirty. My father's blatant affection for my mother never bothered me, but my brothers were a different story.

"Damn, Pops. Get a room," Luke grumbled, provin' my point. Walkin' in with Owen behind him.

"I did. My house, ya feel me?"

"Loud and clear, still fuckin' gross."

"Luke!" Mom reprimanded.

"Fuck isn't a bad word. It's in the dictionary."

She disagreed, "That makes no sense."

"It does in my head."

I scoffed out a chuckle, bringin' his attention over to me. "You gonna let her ride out like that?"

"There is nothin' wrong with my dress, *baby brother.* Dad says I look beautiful, you cock-blocker."

"Harley Jameson!" Momma chastised.

"What? That's what Daddy says to them. He says they're supposed to be my cock-blockers. Why am I always gettin' in trouble for repeatin' the things he says? But Luke and Owen can say anythin' they want?"

"Cuz we got big dic—"

The glare in Momma's eyes was enough to render Owen speechless.

This was the norm in my house, and I wouldn't have it any other way.

By the time we arrived at Memaw's restaurant that Uncle Noah had rented out for the night, everyone was already there, except for the guest of honor, Aunt Skyler. Who had no idea he was surprisin' her with this party for their anniversary. I, for one, couldn't wait to see her reaction.

Memaw closed down the restaurant for the private party, transformin' it into an elegant space. Yellow linen tables surrounded the dance floor and stage, while twinklin' lights hung from the ceilin', addin' the perfect touch to their romantic event.

A huge cake sat on the table in the corner, just waitin' to be eaten. I may have been all Jameson, but I still had the Ryder sweet tooth from my momma.

It was all going to be super romantic.

There was just somethin' about anniversaries and weddin's that got to my heart, and this was no different. Aunt Skyler was stunned and amazed when she arrived by the love fillin' the room from her family and friends. Uncle Noah even flew in some people from her *Skyler Bell* days.

I resisted the urge to ask for autographs, tryin' to play it cool. However, I snapped a few photos incognito from across the room.

You know, for The Gram.

"Harley, that dress is everything!" Aunt Skyler exclaimed when she saw me.

"I know. I made it awesome."

"Just let me know when to make the call. My finger is already on the send button."

She was constantly sayin' this to Cash and me, wantin' to help us with her industry connections. But we were both adamant on accomplishin' our dreams and goals on our own. It'd mean more than it just bein' handed to us.

"Babe, you have such an eye for fashion."

"She gets it from me," Uncle Noah chimed in, beamin' at her.

"You mean you own more than five white t-shirts, three pairs of jeans, a pair of combat boots, and a cut?" she replied, rustlin' his feathers.

"I got this suit for ya, yeah?"

"I have a feeling it's rented."

I giggled, agreein' with her. He tickled the side of her stomach and pulled her out on the dance floor. I watched as they took the floor front and center. Holdin' each other tight as they danced to their weddin' song.

They looked perfect together.

The way my aunt and uncle stared at each other was something I'd always remember. I'd meet my prince, and I'd have my perfect night too. Hopin' he would look at me the way Uncle Noah looked at her.

Sometimes, it felt like I would never find a love like the couples in my family shared. They all had their own stories, their own battles and obstacles they'd overcome.

Where love prevailed, no matter what.

163

In one way or another, each of their love stories were my favorite. Especially, my parents'.

Where my dad didn't give up…

Until he got *his* girl.

I would forever be waitin' for a love like that of my own. The older I got, the more I realized who I wanted to share my happily ever after with.

Except, it wouldn't be easy. It never was with him. I hated him. I loved him. I wanted him to be mine.

But maybe, just maybe…

He always was.

Our eyes locked from across the dance floor just as that thought crossed my mind. Like a sign from the universe. In a room filled to the brim with people, we found each other without even tryin' or lookin'.

As if our souls just connected.

The expression on Jackson's face was one I hadn't seen before. I never wanted to know what he was thinkin' more than I did in that second.

Did he like my dress?

My hair?

My makeup?

Most importantly, why did I care?

Suddenly, Jason Mraz's song "I Won't Give Up" blared through the speakers and he started walkin' toward me.

"I can see your wheels spinnin', Harley. What's got your mouse runnin'?"

My eyes snapped to Cash, but I was too late. He was already followin' my gaze to what held me captive.

Causin' him to jerk back. "Jackson?"

"What?"

Jackson had stopped dead in his tracks, givin' me time to recover.

"No. I was lookin' at the cake behind him."

Cash eyed me skeptically, though he didn't call me out on it. Instead, he reached out his hand and simply said, "Dance wit' me, Harley."

I bit my lip, wantin' to look back at Jackson but aware Cash would know somethin' was up.

What was happenin' between us?

Pushin' the thought away from my mind, I stated the truth, "I've never slow danced with a boy before. My daddy might kill you."

164

"I can handle your old man."

I smirked, givin' into his request. I grabbed his hand. "In that case, I'd love to."

He led us to the dance floor and molded me close to his body, pullin' me tighter into his strong chest.

"Look at you, Cash. Is this how you score with all the girls at our school?"

He winked, guidin' my arms up around his neck.

I squealed like a girl, impressed with his moves. "You lead?"

Ignorin' my question, he chose that second to spin me around, and it was then I realized we'd grabbed the attention of the whole room. Momma was holdin' Daddy back and Aunt Skyler was doin' the same with Uncle Noah. Allowin' me to have this moment with my best friend.

Content, I leaned my face into his chest and slow danced with him. It was around the chorus of the song when something felt different.

He felt different.

And I wasn't referrin' to the boy I was dancin' with.

I swear I felt him starin' at us, burnin' a hole into my heart. All the conflictin' emotions came tumblin' down on me the further the lyrics of the melody intensified. Feelin' like Jackson was singin' them to me.

"We had to learn how to bend without the world caving in on us."

Cash spun me again.

"I had to learn what I got, and what I'm not and who I am without you in my life."

We swayed to the beat, in sync with one another. The room closin' in on us. It wasn't until the last chorus when the lyrics really hit home.

"Giving you all my love, I'm still holding on. Cause God you're worth it."

I wasn't just imaginin' things, it was clear as day. Fuelin' all these emotions I couldn't describe, or even begin to understand.

Jackson's vicious bullyin'.

His lost eyes.

His sad soul.

His, his, his…

What the hell was goin' on?

"Thanks for the dance, Harley."

When I opened my eyes, I stared straight in the direction where I felt Jackson's presence.

Thinkin'.

Hopin'.

Waitin'.
For him to be right there.
Except I was wrong, cuz...

He wasn't.

Chapter Twenty-Four

Jackson

I took an Uber back home, leaving the party early. Lying my ass off to Noah and Skyler I wasn't feeling well, but it was complete bullshit. I couldn't stay there for another fuckin' second. I was livid, pissed beyond belief, and I couldn't even tell you why.

I just was.

Harley looked so different, nothing like the girl I'd known all my life. Between her hair, makeup, heels, and stupid strapless dress, she was almost unrecognizable. It was the first time her appearance caught my attention for a completely different reason.

The Gremlin made my cock twitch.

Before I knew what I was doing, I was snapping photos of her with my phone. Unable to stop myself.

Giving the word *creeper* a whole new definition.

Yet there I was, staring at the images I took of her on the drive home. I couldn't help myself.

What the fuck is going on with me?

For a moment tonight, she had me. Like really fuckin' had me. I was making my way toward her when Cash cock blocked me like the little bitch he was.

Every time I pictured his arms around her.

Touching her skin.

Feeling her warmth.

Her head on his chest.

The way they moved together as if they were made for each

other…

Fucked with me until I saw nothing but red.

I wanted to punch his lights out, bury him alive. The irrational thoughts were taking me hostage, and I was right there along for the ride. Hanging on by an extremely thin thread. Ready for it to snap any second.

My blood was boiling, feeling fury in every inch of my skin in a way I'd never experienced before. I wanted to hurt somebody.

Him.

Cash 'fuckin' McGraw.

I hated him more than I hated Harley.

Once the driver announced, "We're here." I realized I'd spent the last thirty minutes thinking only of them.

They consumed my mind, and it felt like it'd only just started.

Stepping out of the car, I walked inside my house.

Instantly hearing Journey shout, "Ma! Ma! Ma!" from her nursery.

I barely had time to register what she said because the next voice I heard came from the person I'd least expected…

My father.

"This is what you wanted all along, isn't it?! To take my family from me!" he viciously spewed in a tone I'd never heard before.

Who was he yelling at?

I didn't have to wonder who it was for long, because Mary Poppins quickly defended herself, "That's absurd! I'm just trying to help, and you're doing the exact opposite of that right now!"

The string I was hanging onto pulled me in the direction of their voices, one foot in front of the other.

Four steps.

Six steps.

Seven.

Eight.

Nine.

"Journey, come to Daddy!"

"Ma! Ma! Ma!"

He's here… he's really fuckin' here.

Nineteen steps.

Twenty-five.

Thirty-one.

My heart was pounding louder and harder. Faster and faster with no end in sight.

His voice boomed off the walls and the doorway I was now standing in. "She's not your mother!" he roared with the same rage I felt for him since my mom left us.

With no thought, no hesitation, no problem whatsoever, I sneered, "She's the only mother Journey's ever known!"

Both their glares snapped over to me, and I watched him come face-to-face with his reality.

I mirrored his demeanor, his composure, his downright arrogance.

Man against man.

Son versus father.

Love with hate.

There was no denying how much I fuckin' hated him.

"What did you just say?" he questioned in an eerie, menacing tone. One that had Camila holding Journey more firmly in her protective arms.

"You heard me," I bit, my fists clenching at my sides. "But I have no problem saying it to you again." Stepping up to his face, I eyed him up and down.

Finally.

I could say what I'd been holding in.

For my brother.

My sister.

My mother.

The family we used to be. The love we used to share. All the admiration and respect I once held for him was gone in an instant.

I didn't hold back, snarling, "She's the only mother Journey's ever known. The only father she's ever known as well."

He grimaced, not hiding his reaction from me.

Good.

Because I was only getting started.

"You don't know her, and I'm not talking about Camila. Journey loves her, unlike you, who doesn't know the meaning of the word."

He didn't say a thing, not one fuckin' word. Adding fuel to the fire I felt deep in my bones.

"You're nothing like the man I thought you were. My hero, my father, my best fucking friend…"

His jaw hardened as he held his head higher. His strong composure, disintegrating right in front of my eyes.

I grinned, feeling an intense satisfaction I was hurting him, savoring the emotion it enticed. Knowing I was getting through to him.

"After everything you promised Mom, Jagger, me, *your* family… you're just like them. You're exactly like the men who didn't give a shit about you."

His hands fisted at his sides, his temper threatening near the surface.

We were one and the same, but this would be a battle I'd win. Even if I killed both of us.

"How's it feel to turn out a piece of shit like them? Huh? How's it feel to lose everything you worked so hard for?" I mocked, fully aware this was slaying him. Comparing him to the worthless bastards who'd shit on him foster house after foster house he was placed in.

"Jackson, that's enough," Camila uttered in a soft voice, not wanting this war to reach a point of no return.

Glaring solely at my father, I snidely replied, "You're not my mother. She's gone, and she's not coming back."

He was teetering on the edge. I could physically see him hanging on by a thread.

"Jackson, please, just stop."

"Oh, come on, Mary Poppins! Don't you want to know where she is? I thought that's what you wanted!"

We both jerked back when he finally spoke, "Jackson Pierce, don't talk to her like that. I raised you better than this. You want to come at me, then you come at me like a man. Leave her out of this!"

"Oh…" I cocked my head to the side. "For Camila, you talk, huh? Mom would love that."

"Jacks—"

"And you haven't raised me for almost a year!" I reminded him. "All you give a fuck about is your goddamn hospital!"

"Watch your mouth," he warned, getting closer to me.

"Oh, so you want to try to be my father now? Where the fuck has he been while everyone else has taken care of his responsibilities? Huh?!" I shoved him, not giving a fuck about the consequences of putting my hands on him.

He didn't waver, not that I expected him to.

"You think I need you? You think I want you in my life? I don't give a shit about you! Do you hear me?" I pushed him again, much harder. "Do you understand me? I don't give one flying fuck about you! To hell with you!"

Taking one last look at him, I stated the truth, "You're nothing but a sorry excuse of a man who abandoned his kids when they needed him the most!"

Camila gasped at the same time his hand flew back.

"No!" she yelled just as he backhanded me across the face.

My head whooshed back, taking half of my body with me. Journey burst into a fit of tears, screaming at the top of her lungs again.

He instantly reached for me, but I forcefully shoved his arms away. Even the sorrowful expression that fell upon his face meant shit to me.

"Jackson, I didn't mean to do that! You know I would never hurt you! I would die before I ever hurt you," he profoundly apologized in his own way, his eyes filling with regret and devastation all at once.

"Shhh… it's okay, Journey, it's alright," Camila soothed my baby sister, who was screaming in her arms.

I stared in the eyes of the man I used to know. The father I admired, loved, and would have died for.

My stomach somersaulted, making me weak in the knees. The emotions were running so high, you could choke on them, making it hard to fuckin' breathe.

In the blink of an eye, his face changed as if he was examining my appearance, searching for the boy who once loved him more than anything in this world.

He's gone.

And you did that.

I bit back the bile rising in my throat. Briefly blinded by the overwhelming anguish you could feel in the air. With tears blurring my eyes, I looked back at him. Also looking for the father I still wanted more than anything.

"Please stop," Camila repeated, locking stares with me. "You have to stop. Your mom wouldn't have wanted this. No mother would."

My eyes glazed over, triggering something deep inside of me.

She was right.

She wouldn't have wanted this, and for that reason alone, I stopped. Seeing my mother standing in front of me instead of the woman who'd been there for us in her absence all these months.

I blinked, shifting my focus back to him, who was taking in what she had just said as well. Neither of us spoke. Even Journey stopped crying.

The end.

Game over.

I said my piece.

Slowly, I backed away before I turned and left. Leaving open wounds that may never be healed by the hands of the good doctor.

I thought this was what I wanted, what I needed, what I craved.

I was wrong.

I didn't hate him.

I loved him.

But it hurt…

Just the same.

Chapter Twenty-Five

Harley

"We gotta go," Aunt Skyler came runnin' up to Uncle Noah who was sittin' next to me.

"What's goin' on?" he asked, takin' the words out of my mouth.

"It's Aiden. He just called me, he fucked up. We gotta go."

Noah stood, and I found myself standin' with him. Sayin', "I'm comin' too."

Aunt Skyler didn't question me, she just nodded as if she already knew my reasonin'. What I'd been askin' myself since Jackson left the party.

With a heavy foot on the gas, it didn't take long for us to arrive at the Pierces' home. Uncle Noah sped the entire way there, breakin' several laws in the process. All of us stressin' over the anxiety of what was to come. I knew one thing and one thing only, Uncle Aiden hadn't stepped foot in that house since his wife had died.

With my thoughts focused solely on Jackson, I moved in an autopilot state of mind, slammin' the car door behind me. Rushin' right into their house, I darted up the stairs toward his bedroom. My heart feelin' fuller with every stride I made. A thin thread pullin' me, gettin' closer and closer to the boy who might have needed me the most.

Truth was, I had no clue.

The older we became, the more our relationship evolved into something more intense, something unexpected. We both played games, pranks, and fought.

It was our dynamic.

Our understandin'.

Our hate.

It was simple.

Until… it wasn't.

"Jackson?" I knocked on his door.

Silence.

"I'm comin' in."

Nothin'.

Openin' the door, I was careful not to startle him in case he was in his own little world. A place I'd caught him lost in more times than I could remember. The unknown land that I knew tormented him.

The list was endless.

His mom.

His dad.

His mind.

This time, I didn't have to wonder where he was. The window was open, allowing the night breeze to softly blow the sheer curtains aside.

In three steps, I was standin' in front of the windowsill, ready for the battle that was Jackson Pierce. He wouldn't like me bein' here for him, probably thinkin' I would hang it over his head later.

Use it as a weapon, instead of him realizin' I was just tryin' to be his friend.

I'd never personally experienced what he was goin' through. There were things I wouldn't be able to comprehend, emotions I couldn't relate to, fears no one should have to live with.

But in the end, it didn't matter.

I was here for him, nonetheless.

Takin' off my heels, I stepped onto the threshold like he showed me before. Reachin' for the branch to grab to pull myself up. Makin' sure I held on really tight. The last thing I wanted was to plummet to my death, or even worse, rip my new dress.

As if readin' my mind, Jackson hissed, "The fuck, Gremlin?"

"Well, why don't you help me, so I don't fall?"

"What other choice did you leave me, you brat?" He reached for my arm and I gripped onto his hand. In less than a second, I was standin' in front of him, unprepared with what to say or do.

I didn't really think about this part. I went with what felt right, hopin' he would think it was too.

"What are you doing here?" he snapped in the same vicious attitude. Nothin' new.

"I'm here for you."

He narrowed his eyes at me, just as confused as I was with what I said.

"I didn't ask you to come up here."

"You didn't have to."

Jerking back at my response, he followed it up with, "I don't want you here, Harley."

I didn't hesitate in replyin', "Yes you do, Jackson."

"The only thing I have to say to you, Gremlin, is you need to learn how to mind your own fuckin' business. How many times do I have to tell you? I'm sick of this bullshit."

"Why do you do that?" I muttered under my breath. "Why do you always push me away when you're hurtin'?"

"Fuck you, Harley."

"I ain't leavin'. You can use me as your punchin' bag, be mean to me, scream at me. I'll take it all, but after you're done takin' your anger out on me, I'll still be here, cuz I care about you."

His eyes glazed over. It was quick, but I saw it.

"Are you okay, Jackson? Did your father hit you? Your cheek is all red."

"How do you know he's here?"

"He called Skyler, sayin' he fucked up. Is that what he did? Is that why you're up here hidin'?"

"I'm not hiding."

"Alone then."

"I'm not alone anymore. You're here, being a pain in my ass." He abruptly turned, sittin' back down on the middle of the roof.

Followin' his lead, I quickly sat down next to him.

"I'm sorry your dad hit you, but you know he didn't mean it. He loves you. He's just hurtin' cuz of your mom."

"I don't want to talk about it, Harley."

"Okay," I nodded. "We can just sit here and look at the sky."

To say I was shocked when he stated, "I'd like that," and leaned into my embrace would be an understatement.

We stayed there for I don't know how long.

Waitin' for I don't know what.

Jackson

Fuckin' Gremlin.

This day, this night… it went from one thing to another. I couldn't keep up with it anymore. I never expected him to be here, let alone her.

Why was she here?

Why did it feel right?

Why was she dancing with Cash?

My head was pounding, a splitting headache wreaking so much havoc on my mind I could barely see straight. The sting on my cheek didn't help the throbbing in my brain.

I could smell Harley's strawberry hair, her vanilla-scented skin, and cherry lip shit.

She was a beacon of smells, only fuckin' with my other head.

"Did you like dancing with Cash, baby girl?"

It was her turn to jerk back, stunned I went there. "What does he gotta do with anythin'?"

"Everything. He clearly wants to fuck you."

She gasped, glaring at me. "Take that back!"

"Fuck no."

"Why do you do this?"

"Do what exactly? Tell you the truth. Like how ugly your dress is. I don't know what surprises me more—the fact you think your body can actually fill it out, or your daddy letting you leave the house wearing it."

"You're just bein' an asshole to get me to leave."

"Is it working?"

"I saw you starin' at me. I saw where your eyes went. You like my dress, you dick!"

"Staring at what? There's nothing to look at. Try again once you grow some tits."

Her mouth dropped open.

"What, baby girl? Want me to stick my tongue in there again?"

"Jackson… don't do this." She tried to hug me, but I couldn't take the emotional turmoil anymore. I lost my shit on her. "I told you I didn't want you here."

"It's too late for that! I'm here, and I wanna be."

"Then what do I have to say to make you go away?"

"I left Cash to come here, didn't I? For *you*."

"That's not good enough."

"Will anythin' ever be good enough for you?"

"Not when it comes to you."

"What the fuck does that mean?"

"Harley, if you want me to kiss you, touch you, all you gotta do is ask. Putting on a slutty dress won't make me want you."

"It's not a slutty dress! Trust me, I would know. You must have me confused with one of your cheerleadin' brainless groupies."

"There's no confusion, Gremlin. They all have tits and an ass." I looked her up and down. "We both know *you* don't have either."

"You know what? Be alone. But know this, Rudolph... *you* did this. *You* pushed me away. *You* treated me like shit when I was just tryin' to be here for you. You want to live by yourself? Never let anyone in? Why? Huh? Ever ask yourself that, tough guy?!"

"Harley, *don't*."

"Don't what? Huh? Tell you the truth? You think I'm so stupid and naive, your perfect little play toy... you think I don't know you're scared, that you live life in fear of the unknown."

"Harley, I'm warning you. Don't fuck with me."

She stood, hovering. "You think I don't know you have nightmares?! That I don't know you're constantly thinkin' about your mom... but it's so much more than that. You push everyone away cuz you're terrified of losin' someone else who matters to you! Someone else who you care about... think about... fuckin' might love!"

I jumped up, getting right in her face, and before I could say one word, she kneed me in the balls.

"Goddamn it, Harley!"

"I prefer if you don't talk. It's my turn and you'll listen, and you'll listen good, you asshole! *You*, Jackson Pierce, are the reason *I hate you*. Do you understand me? You fucked this up, not me." With that, she turned and left.

Breathing through the pain, I took off after her. Catching up to her once she was in the kitchen, I grabbed her arm and spun her to face me.

"Let's get one thing straight, Harley Jameson. I don't need *you* to check on me. I don't need *you* to tell me what I need. I had a mother for that, and she's fuckin' gone just like everyone I love will be. I don't need anyone. I didn't invite *you* here, you forced your way in." I tugged her to my chest, whispering in her ear, "And if I needed a play toy, it

177

wouldn't be *you*."

"Jackson Pierce!" she screamed, shoving me hard. "I can't believe I wasted my time coming here for you! I hate you!"

"Good! Cuz I can't fuckin' stand you!"

"The fuck is goin' on here?" Noah exclaimed, charging in through the garage door. "Can't leave you two alone for a few minutes without you tearin' into each other. Harley, why did you want to come with us in the first place?"

Her chest was rising and falling, her nostrils flaring.

Skyler walked in behind him, shifting her eyes from Harley to me, back to her again. A knowing expression taking over her entire face.

"Noah, it's been an overwhelming night for us all."

Harley didn't miss a beat, answering his question, "I was wrong to come here. I don't know what I was thinkin'. Can someone take me back to the party, please? Cash is waitin' for me."

I swallowed hard, feeling that sentence in the pit of my stomach. I wish I could say I learned my lesson that night, but I didn't. Not in the least.

What happened next…

Proved that theory.

Chapter Twenty-Six

Jackson

I didn't sleep for shit that night, tossing and turning with no end in sight. My mind consumed with thoughts of my father.

Would he be coming back?

Would things change?

Would he be the man he once was for us?

Journey and Jagger needed him. And maybe, just maybe…

I still did too.

"Jackson!" Mary Poppins shouted through the door, knocking on it.

"Go away!"

"We need to talk!"

"No, we don't!"

"Jackson, please! Just ope—"

Abruptly, I swung the door open. Mostly just to get her out of my face. "What?!"

She jumped back, not expecting me to be so abrasive. "I just wanted to see how you were doing. You don't have to bite my head off."

"I'm fine," I calmly remarked.

I wasn't, but she didn't need to know that.

"You don't look fine."

"What do you want me to say? I'll say whatever to make you go away," I repeated the same thing I'd said to Harley the night before.

She snapped, "What the hell, man?! You're worse than a moody teenage chick! You can't be nice to me and then—"

"Nice to you?" I intervened, taken back. "When was I nice to you?"

"Last night, you defended me to your fath—"

"I did that for Journey, not for you."

"Oh, come on, Jackson. Even you don't believe that. Why can't you just admit you like me? That maybe we could be friends, especially now that I liv—" She stopped herself.

"What?"

"Nothing."

"Don't give me that shit. What were you about to say?"

"Well...what had happened was... last night, I umm... drank a little too much... and uh... didn't make wise choices," she stumbled over her words, one right after the other.

What the hell was going on?

"What does that have to do with what you were about to say?"

I was over the games. I had enough of that with Harley.

"Speak, woman!"

She shrugged. "I kind of live here now."

What the fuck?

"Not forever! It's not like that. Just until I can figure it all out. Honestly, everything just kind of happened really fast and your dad is—"

"An asshole."

"I was going to say protective and stubborn." She nodded. "But your adjective works too."

"My dad moved you in?"

"No."

"No?"

"Maybe. You're confusing me with your trickery, like your dad did this morning."

"This morning? He spent the night with you?"

"What? No!"

"No?"

"Well, kind of, but not like that. You're twisting it again."

"I'm not twisting shit. I'm going off of what you're saying."

Between yesterday and today, I swear I was already losing my mind. She went on about what happened, and I tried to pay attention as best I could. Though she was just as confusing as Harley was.

"So, what you're saying is you got shitfaced, hooked up—"

She interrupted me, going on and on about one thing or another.

Until I finally questioned, "Are you okay?"

She was surprised I followed it up with that, and I'd be lying if I said I wasn't as well.

"Yeah, for the most part. I didn't want any of this to come about, and I feel horrible because it did. Your dad thinks I'm in danger if I stay in my apartment, and he might be right. At this point, I honestly don't know."

"So 'Don't Answer' is that bad?"

She could see the remorse in my eyes.

Why was I feeling so much toward her?

"I mean, I didn't think so until I realized how he's always treated me. Jackson, it's hard to explain. I didn't grow up like you."

I considered what she said for a few seconds, and before I knew what I was saying, I snidely remarked, "I'm sure my mom would love you living here."

She sighed, stepping away, but I grabbed her arm stopping her.

"I didn't mean that. I mean… I did mean that, just not in the asshole way I said it. My mom wouldn't want you to be in danger either. Besides, you stay over most of the time anyway. She'd be happy you're here. For Journey."

She nodded, not knowing what to say.

"And for Jagger."

"And for you?"

I grinned. "Don't push it."

It was the truth. After everything she'd done for us, if she was in danger, then she belonged here too.

"Don't let it go to your head, Mary Poppins. I mostly just like your cooking."

"I thought you accused me of trying to poison you?"

"That's probably true."

"Probably, huh? Did you probably help me last night because you kind of like me too?"

"I already told you, I did that for Journey."

"Well, whatever the reason, thank you."

"You're not going to get all mushy and want to hug me, right?"

She laughed. "I don't know, Jackson. Maybe we should hug it out. Maybe you're a closet hugger and you just don't know it yet."

"Ask Harley. She'll tell you what happened after she tried to hug me last night too."

"Aww. I saw you guys on the roof. You were so cute, I think you lov—"

"Finish that sentence and watch how fast I slam the door in your face. She caught me at a moment of weakness, it's not going to happen again."

It wasn't. It couldn't. I wouldn't allow it.

"Maybe it will."

"I'm positive it won't."

"Why are you so mean to her?"

"Cuz I can't stand her."

"If that were true, you never would've let her comfort you in the first place."

"I was thinking with the wrong head."

"Ugh!" She stepped back. "I'm going to pretend you didn't just say that."

"Then you shouldn't have asked."

"I'm going to go now. Are we cool?"

"I'm not happy about you being the one who told me you're living here now. But it has nothing to do with you and everything to do with him."

"Jackson, give him a break. I'm sure he was going to tell you. I just beat him to it. He had to go to the hospital."

"After the way he treated you last night, you're still defending him?"

Why was it so easy for people to forgive him?

What was it about my father that had an effect on people?

"Journey keeps calling me 'Ma', and every time it comes out of her mouth it hurts my heart. I can't imagine what it feels like for your dad to hear her say it."

"What does he expect?" I nodded, feeling that statement in my conscience. "He's never around. Journey is with you all the time. I could think of worse things she could say."

"Especially with what comes out of your mouth."

I chuckled. More truth.

"Your dad loves you, Jackson. I know that sounds really hard to believe right now, but it's accurate. He wouldn't have asked me to move in if he didn't love you as much as he does."

"What does that have to do with anything?"

"Because it's the first thing that flew out of his mouth this morning. What you guys would say to him if something happened to me. See, even he knows you like me."

"You're reaching, Camila."

"You called me Camila, not Mary Poppins. Hashtag progress."

I shook my head. "You really need to stop watching *Mean Girls*."

"I'm not a regular nanny." She smirked, winking. "I'm a cool nanny."

Rolling my eyes, I hid back a smile. Enjoying the fact, we were establishing some sort of middle ground.

"Better watch out, cool nanny, who knows what I'm going to do to you now that you live here."

She stopped smirking. "Wait, what?"

I deviously grinned before shutting and locking the door.

"Jackson!" She banged on it. "This is BS! You can't keep pranking me!"

No answer, I pretended as if I couldn't hear her. Already planning in my head what was in store for her. It was a nice distraction from the bullshit all around me.

"I know you can hear me! This works both ways, you demon spawn! I will get you back and really poison your food, so that you're shitting for weeks!"

"Good to see you guys are back to normal," Jagger interrupted, while I listened to him through the wood barrier.

"Oh my God, Jagger! How do you just keep showing up out of nowhere? How long have you been standing there?"

"Long enough to know you're moving in."

"It's not like—"

"I know what it's like. It's *you* that doesn't."

What did he mean by that?

"You're like a fortune cookie, care to elaborate?"

"Nah, it's more entertaining watching you figure it out for yourself."

"Watching me figure what out?"

"You'll see."

"Jagger, I know you're a guy of very few words, but with the words you do use, can they please make sense?"

"They will, eventually."

"Again, with the cryptic messages."

Skyler interrupted them, and I moved away from the door. Climbing out my window instead.

I sat on the roof for the rest of day, contemplating what was going to happen next.

Between my father and Harley, I had a lot on my mind, remembering the words I'd said to both of them the night prior.

I don't know what I hated more…

That I'd hurt them.

Or, that it hurt me doing so.

Chapter Twenty-Seven

Jackson

Then: Sixteen years old

The more things changed, the more they stayed the same.

Over the last two and a half years, my life drastically took a turn mostly for the better but some things for the worse.

"Jackson! Are you weady? Wook at me! I wook so prewty!" Journey exclaimed, clumsily twirling for me in her white flower girl dress.

"You look just like a princess."

She beamed with her precious smile. "Dis what I wanted!"

"You nailed it, baby sister."

"I ain't a *baby* no more. I treee and a haff." She held up three fingers. "Dis many."

I nodded. "Such a big girl."

"See... I prewty and know everyting."

"Just like me."

She giggled, agreeing with me. "Will you dance wif me?"

"Of course."

"Like dis?" She put her hands on her knees and got down low, just like Camila had taught her.

It was their thing, booty dancing together all around the house.

Driving my father crazy because she was teaching Journey her Latina ways.

I laughed. I couldn't help it. She was cute as fuck.

"I dance wif Cash too. He my boyfrwend."

"Is that right?"

She giggled again and took off running toward Camila's bridal suite. "Ma! Ma! Ma!" she shouted, as loud as could be barreling down the hall.

I sighed, shaking my head.

Ever since we watched the movie *Coco* together, she was obsessed with the guitar playing hero. A few days later, we went to the MC barbeque on Sunday and Cash just happened to be playing. Cue instant crush.

The motherfucker knew it too.

Her eyes literally lit up, and he spent the next hour showing her how to strum a couple chords. Everyone thought it was adorable, except for me. Thank fuck they were twelve years apart, or I'd really have to kill the son of a bitch.

We hated each other more now than ever before.

Fuckin' Gremlin and her Scooby Doo gang were tighter than ever as well. Even pussy boy had his own following. His talentless band started making a name for themselves in Oak Island, playing at all our school events and town functions. It was beyond pathetic to watch girls throw themselves at them.

The girl I still hated the most, Harley Jameson, was still his number one fan.

Our relationship, or should I say our hatred for one another, hadn't changed. In fact, it had only got worse the older we got. Noah and Skyler's anniversary party may have brought my father home, but it caused Harley to run further away from me.

She was right.

I did fuck it up.

It was just easier that way.

I hid my anger the only way I knew how, terrorizing the shit out of her and Mary Poppins. However, now... I really did bring a different girl home every week. Being the most popular guy at our high school, I had a reputation to uphold. I took it very fuckin' serious.

I was the star quarterback, a fuckin' God among mortals.

I'd be stupid not to take advantage of the endless pussy thrown my way on the daily. I wasn't lying to Harley that night on the roof. I'd never use her as my play toy.

She was everything but that.

Trigger didn't help the situation by any means. He wouldn't stop sniffing around Shiloh, who still didn't give two fucks about him. She blew him off every chance she got.

The whole football team and I found it hilarious to witness, certainly a sight to see. It didn't stop him though. If anything, it made him want her more. Once and for all, proving he could get any girl he chased like the alpha he was.

Which was the biggest difference between Trigger and I, he pursued girls and I didn't. They just flocked to me. I was a teenage guy with needs, and they were more than eager to get on their knees. Wanting to score my letterman jacket and the title of my girlfriend.

Fuck that.

I allowed them to swallow my cum instead.

And they did just that.

What had completely changed in my life was my old man. After he moved Mary Poppins in, everything went from zero to a hundred in the blink of an eye.

Including my love, appreciation, and gratitude for her.

For the first time in over a year, my father finally came home. He stepped back up to the plate and made it known he'd royally fucked up. Abandoning us when we needed him the most.

His reasoning.

His struggle.

His story…

Was *his* to tell.

All I knew was I had my dad in my life again, and nothing was better than that. The father figure I grew up with, the man I aspired to become one day, came back with a vengeance. Verifying he was still my hero.

The night all my pent-up emotions exploded on him like a volcano was truly a blessing in disguise. He'd needed to hear every last word, and I'd needed to say it. Burning him alive, purging all the hatred I had for the man in a matter of minutes. It was what changed our dynamic from that day forward. Little by little, he redeemed himself to his children. Confirming he did love us more than anything after all.

Every family had ups and downs, and we were no different. Bottom line… where there was love, there was hope.

Which brought us to the big day, all thanks to the woman who'd changed our lives. He was marrying his second soulmate in a whirlwind ceremony, and I couldn't have been happier for them.

Once he told Camila the truth about my mother and her whereabouts, their relationship grew to love. Mary Poppins was made for him, and in many ways, she saved us all. After much consideration, it was evident we couldn't continue living in a house that held my mother's presence in every room. There were too many memories lingering within the walls of our home. Not only for our father, but also for my brother and me.

We all had needed a fresh start, especially after we cleaned out her belongings.

It hurt. A lot.

"Maybe we should keep these for Journey," Jagger suggested, holding up a few pieces of her jewelry, photos, and her wedding gown that afternoon.

"I think that's a great idea," Camila replied.

"The rest we can donate to a charity for dementia?" Jagger added, setting those things aside.

"Your mom would love that. What do you think, Jackson?"

"I don't care. Do what you want with it."

"You boys should keep whatever you want as well," Camila suggested, staring only at me.

I didn't pay her any mind, grabbing one of the boxes that was full. "I don't need anything," I stated, wholeheartedly meaning it. "Makes no difference to me."

I already owned what mattered most to her. The necklace I broke off her neck years ago. The one that belonged to her mother before she passed.

No one knew I had possession of it.

I walked out of the room to take a few boxes to the garage when I heard Jagger whisper, "I will make him a box."

It hadn't taken us long to find a new home. It was massive, nine bedrooms, eleven bathrooms, a private guesthouse in the back, where both occupancies overlooked the lake.

There was plenty of space for the shitlins I knew they'd be having soon. My father was going to knock Camila up once that wedding band was on her finger.

They both wanted a bigger family.

Bigger than what we already had, and she was still young. He didn't hold back on the cost of this wedding either, which didn't surprise me. It was always how he showed his love and devotion. Spending his hard-earned money on those he cared about the most, providing the life he'd never had, but always wanted.

"Dad, you ready?" I questioned, walking up to him and Noah.

"I am."

It was blatantly obvious he was.

"I'm happy for you, Dad. You deserve to love again."

"Thank you, Son. You have no idea how much that means to me, coming from you. I know I've said this a thousand times, but I'll never forgive myself for what I put you all through."

I shrugged. "Shit happens."

"Your mother would be so proud of you, Jackson. I hope you know that."

"Mmm hmm."

"You're all she ever wanted."

I scoffed out a chuckle, "Yet she forgot me first."

"Jackson—"

"Let's go get you hitched to a woman who's closer to my age than yours."

Mary Poppins was only fifteen years older than me. My friends were constantly jerking off to her videos and pictures on social media. She was the hottest "Mom" at our school. It pissed my dad off to no end, but it was funny as fuck to watch him lose his shit over it.

Camila and I continued to prank each other every chance we got. Just last week, I brought over my friend's pet tarantula and put it in the bathroom while she was showering.

Of course, I recorded her reaction from right outside their bedroom. The high pitch screaming as she jumped out of the tub, taking the shower curtain with her. Running out of their bedroom soaking wet, hollering, "I'm going to kill you, Jackson Pierce!"

I uploaded it to my YouTube channel straightaway, titling it *Wet And Wild Nanny Exposed.* Gaining over a hundred thousand views within an hour.

I'd say it was a huge success.

I wouldn't call myself a Youtuber, since I only posted whenever the mood spiked, but I definitely made a shit ton of money when I did upload. My content was fucking hilarious.

Art was by far one of my favorite hobbies. Whether it was photography or videography, I had a passion for bringing things to life. Constantly finding inspiration in the places I least expected to.

Although, there was another reason why I took pictures and recorded things. I had a much bigger motive.

That I shared with *no one.*

As soon as Harley saw my old man make his way toward the altar, she started crying. Standing there in her bridesmaid dress, we waited for our turn to walk down the aisle.

"Get it together, Gremlin."

"Shut up, Rudolph."

"It's a wedding, not a funeral. Stop crying."

"Screw you, I'll do what I want."

"Don't make me trip you."

"I swear to God, Jackson, if you make me fall in front of everyone, I will have your balls."

I nodded to her gown. "Maybe it will help your latest disaster." She was wearing the ugliest dress I'd ever seen with her tits out for everyone to see.

Yes, the Gremlin grew a pair of knockers. They were nice ones too, and I resisted the urge to tell her to cover them up.

"Really? Cuz I already have five orders for it on my Etsy Store."

"Those people obviously have no taste."

"You're such a fuckin' asshole."

"Shhh… God's listening." I extended my arm for her to take. "Baby girl, we're up."

"Stop callin' me that."

"But you love it so much."

She glared at me before looping her arm through mine.

190

"Better hold on tight. You might fall in those fuck-me heels."

Shoving me with her shoulder, we walked side-by-side down the aisle. I didn't hesitate in smiling for the guests in attendance, while I slightly shoved her back.

"Jackson, stop," she clenched out.

"Just helping you maintain your balance, so you don't take me down with you in front of all these people."

"I can walk in heels, you dick."

"Stop thinking about my dick, Harley."

Taking a deep breath, she steadied herself, smiling even though she wanted nothing more than to shove me again, or better yet, knee me in my balls.

It was still her favorite thing to do.

On my last step before we went our separate ways, I leaned forward and kissed her cheek.

She instantly gasped, surprised by my not so subtle gesture.

Since the night on the roof, there was something about the combination of her vanilla, strawberry, and cherry scents that made my cock twitch. I just wanted a second to take it in. I'd never admit this to anyone, especially her, but any time I smelled any of those scents, I couldn't help but get hard.

Fuckin' Harley.

The ceremony continued without a problem, their vows were perfectly geared to each other, and it wasn't until the minister said, "By the power vested in me by the state of North Carolina, I now pronounce you husband and wife. Aiden, you may kiss your bride."

That I fully understood we were now officially a family. With a father and a new mother.

Chapter Twenty-Eight

Jackson

Sometime during the evening, Jagger, Journey, and I pulled Camila and our dad to the side to give them our wedding gift. From an outsider looking in, you wouldn't think we weren't biologically hers, not with how she openly showed how much she loved us.

This wasn't our father's idea. It was ours.

"What is this?" she asked when I handed her a manila file with a big red bow on it.

"Open it and find out, Mary Poppins."

"Jackson, if something bursts out of these files and you mess up my dress, I will show the next girl you bring to the house your baby pictures with your ass sticking up in the air."

"Relax," I coaxed. "My next prank isn't until tomorrow. It's an epic one though, so be prepared."

She glared at me in the same way Gremlin always did.

"By the way, this was all of our idea. Not just Journey's and mine. Jackson wanted this too," Jagger emphasized, winking at her.

She opened the file and her mouth dropped open. "If this is a prank, I'm going to kill you," she wept with tears instantly springing in her eyes.

"No, it's not. Journey, Jagger, and I would love for you to officially adopt us. We want you to be our mom. I mean... that's if you wan—"

She cut me off, throwing her arms around my neck.

"Oh, fuck! This is completely unnecessary, Mary Poppins!"

"Shut up, Jackson." She hugged me tighter, pulling Jagger and Journey into her embrace as well.

I let her have this moment, despite still hating being hugged. A whole other reason I'd never shared with anyone.

"I would be honored to be your mom. I love you all so much, and I know I'll never be able to take Bailey's place, but if you'll let me, I'll try to be the best substitute in her absence."

"Ma!" Journey chimed in, hugging her so hard, her eyes closed.

Camila spent a lot of time showing Journey pictures of our mother. She never wanted her not to know who her real mother was. Journey listened, loving her birth story, but in my baby sisters' eyes...

Mary Poppins was her mother.

The night progressed, and at one point, I sat down at the corner table by the dance floor, watching the guests having the time of their lives.

Including Harley, who wouldn't stop dancing.

Her body swayed.

Her ass shook.

Her tits bounced.

She was a fuckin' muse.

I don't know at what point it was where I started gravitating toward her. It was as if I blinked and I was standing in front of her. Reaching my hands out for her to take.

She eyed me up and down, narrowing her bright blue, enticing gaze at me. They were rimmed with black eyeliner, luring me in profusely.

"You're jokin', right? This a prank?"

"Shut up and just dance with me, Gremlin."

"You can dance?"

"I'm standing here, aren't I?"

"I don't trust you."

"That offends me deeply."

"Jackson, I don't wanna play—"

"No games, just dance with me. I'll even say please."

"Are you feelin' okay?"

"I'd feel better if you'd dance with me."

"Fine," she sighed, giving in. "But if you—"

I grabbed her wrists and pulled her tight to my chest. She felt good in my arms.

Damn fuckin' good.

"How do you always smell like that?" I whispered in her ear, slowly starting to dance.

"Smell like what?"

"Edible."

"Are you saying you wanna eat me, Jackson Pierce?"

"Now that's a loaded question if I ever heard one, Harley Jameson."

Her heart began pounding against mine.

"Am I making your heart beat fast?"

"No."

"No?"

"If it's beatin' fast, it's only cuz I'm waitin' for you to do somethin' horrible to me."

"Oh, come on, I'm not that bad."

"You're rotten to the core. What's gotten into you anyway?"

"I don't know. Weddings and all that, I guess. Sunshine and happiness, like Skyler always says."

"Oh... so you're feelin' nostalgic, for what exactly? Cuz I think I saw Willow around here somewhere. I'm sure she'll do whatever you—"

"Fuck her."

"I thought you were."

Willow was Journey's babysitter. My old man hired her over two years ago to help when Mary Poppins went to nursing school.

She'd sucked my cock a few times—nothing more, nothing less.

"I'm not fuckin' her, Harley."

"Oh."

I spun her, bringing her back to me. "Would it bother you if I was?"

194

"No."

"No?"

"Why would it bother me?"

"Why wouldn't it?"

"And, of course, answerin' a question with a question. How I love this game," she sarcastically remarked, making me chuckle.

"Everyone at school thinks you're fuckin' her."

"Everyone at school thinks I'm fuckin' you too."

It was true.

We spent a lot of time together because of our families. It was only natural they assumed something was happening behind closed doors between us.

It was the only rumor I never denied. I don't know why, I just didn't.

She rolled her eyes. "Ugh. Don't remind me. You know it would probably help if you actually said we weren't, so I wouldn't have to keep tellin' people I hate you and we're not doin' it."

"Where would the fun be in that?"

"And by fun, you mean torturin' me?"

"Always."

"Are you ever gonna give me the videos you still have of me?"

"Again, where would the fun be in that, Gremlin?"

"Rudolph, you're so lucky people are around us, or I would have kneed you in the balls by now."

"Since when has that ever stopped you?"

For the reason of knowing her better than she knew herself, I blocked her knee toward my boys and tugged her closer to me. Leaving no room in between us.

"I hate you so much."

"Ditto, you fuckin' brat."

"What do ya want?"

"Can't a guy just dance with his girl?"

"I ain't your girl."

"Harley." I grinned. "If that were true, then people wouldn't assume I've been balls deep inside of you."

"Gross. Just the thought of that makes me wanna puke on you."

"Trust me, Toots, I can make you gag." I thrusted my cock into her core.

"Ugh. You're disgustin'. I hope my dad saw that."

"Your dad took your mom into one of the rooms. They're busy fuc—"

"Jackson, you're so vulgar!"

I smiled, snidely mocking, "Your dad took your mom into one of the rooms to plow into her fruity tooty. Better?'

"Hardly. I can't believe you even remember that."

"I remember everything when it comes to you."

"And why's that?"

"Cuz I hate you."

"Alrighty then, this was a great talk. Let's do this *never* again."

She went to leave as the music switched over to Jason Mraz's "I Won't Give Up".

I fuckin' despised this song, remembering back to the night of Noah and Skyler's anniversary party.

"Rudolph, let go of me."

"I'm not done dancing with you."

"You don't own me. Let go."

"I could always show your dad my latest video. You know, the one where you're sneaking out of your room to come to mine."

"You arrogant dick! I was not comin' into your room for anythin' other than gettin' my homework you stole from me to hand in as yours."

"Considering you wrote a paper about me, I needed to make sure you weren't making me look bad."

"You do enough of that on your own. And it wasn't a paper about you."

"It was titled 'Jackson Pierce'."

"The topic was to write about someone you'd save durin' a zombie apocalypse. I just put my own twist on it, feedin' you to flesh eatin' monsters first."

"Says the girl who took cover behind me when we played paint ball last week."

"Yeah. So, they would hit *you*. Not me."

I chuckled, fuckin' brat.

"You just want me to protect you."

"If I needed protection, you'd be the last person I'd ever go to."

"Keep telling yourself that and maybe you'll eventually start to believe it. Besides, I don't have to show him that video. I can show him the one of you wearing that skimpy piece of fuckin' string you wore to the beach—"

She gasped. "You recorded me in my pink bikini?"

"Amongst other things."

"That takes this creeper thing to another level, Jackson! You better not use it for your spank bank."

"Too late."

Her mouth dropped open. I hadn't, but she didn't have to know that. I loved pissing her off, it was funny.

"If you're gonna wear next to nothing, then I'm gonna use it to my advantage."

"You are disgustin'!" she restated, her face turning bright red.

"Harley, I see the books you read, you dirty girl."

"Oh my God! I knew I saw you lookin' in my bedroom."

"You leave the drapes open, so I will."

"In your dreams, you creeper."

"I gotta fuck my fist since I'm not fuckin' anyone else."

She jerked back by my statement. "What?"

"You heard me."

"You're not fuckin' anyone else, *now*?"

"I've never fucked anyone else, *ever*."

"You're lyin'."

"No, but I will if you ever repeat that."

"You want me to believe you're a virgin?"

"I prefer to think of it as being selective as fuck. My cock is too precious. It deserves the best."

"You're so full of shit."

"Why would I lie?"

"I don't know. To make me think you're a decent guy. Girls at school talk, Jackson. I ain't stupid."

"I fuck their faces, not their pussies. If they want to say otherwise, that's on them."

Her gaze zeroed in on me, and I spun her again before she stressed, "I still don't believe you."

I pulled her close to my chest, muttering in her ear, "I swear on my mother's grave."

She winced, finally believing me. "Why?"

"Why not?"

"No. Answer my question. Why are you still a virgin? You could have any girl."

"I don't want *any* girl."

"That makes no sense. You're Jackson Pierce, you're a God in this town."

"I prefer legend."

"Whatever. Why ain't you sleepin' around like everyone says you are?"

"I got better things to do."

"Like what?"

I winked. "Dance with you."

She didn't say a word, taking in everything I just shared.

"It's not that shocking. My mom did raise me to be a gentleman, Gremlin. I want it to be with someone who deserves my dick."

Her eyes widened. "You sound like a chick."

"Are you calling me a pussy? Cuz I'd love to show you how much of a man I really am."

She swallowed hard. "You wanna sleep with me?"

"I wouldn't call it sleeping."

"Fuck me, then?"

"Are you asking or begging?"

"You know what I mean. Answer my question."

"I thought I just did."

"Why would ya wanna lose your virginity to me?"

"Someone has to take yours."

She challenged, "How do you know someone hasn't already?"

"Don't fuck with me, Harley," I stated in a cocky tone. "We both know you won't win."

"I'd never give you my v-card, Jackson Pierce." I could see it in her eyes, she was going to say something spiteful, but I never expected it to be, "I'd sleep with Cash, who's like a brother to me, before I ever slept with you."

It was my turn to jerk back, hurt.

The chorus of the song kicked up, and the person I least expected stepped up next to us.

"Can I cut in?" Willow requested in a sultry tone.

I didn't think twice about letting go of Harley. "I'd love to dance with you, baby." Shifting my stare back to the Gremlin, looking her up and down, I spoke the truth, "Yeah, I'm done with her."

She glared at me, and I smirked before turning my back to her, leaving her all alone…

On the dance floor.

Chapter Twenty-Nine

Harley

Then: Fifteen years old

I'd been standin' there watchin' them for what felt like forever. Lost in my own thoughts.

What does she have that I don't?

Why do I care?

Why am I thinkin' about him? Them?

Why is it botherin' me that they haven't stopped hangin' out together?

I. Hate. Him.

But why do I now hate her? I don't even know her.

Why does everythin' about her piss me off? From her hair, to her nails, to her dress... even the sound of her voice bothers me.

Don't get me started on the way she looks at him.

Barf.

Why do I feel this way?

His words, "Yeah, I'm done with her." Playin' over and over in my head. Triggerin' the ache in my heart with every word.

"You alright?" Camila asked, catchin' me off guard in the corner of the room.

"Yeah, of course." I shrugged, looking at her. "Why wouldn't I be?"

"You've been staring at them for the last hour."

"Who?" I played dumb.

"Jackson and Willow."

"I think you're seein' things."

"It's okay, Harley, you don't have to pretend with me."

"What are you sayin'?"

"I'm saying I know you don't hate him."

"Pshhh... that's funny, Camila. I can't stand him."

She arched an eyebrow, cocking her head to the side as if she was calling my bluff.

"What? I do."

"Hate is a strong word, sweetheart."

"Yeah. One that perfectly describes my feelings toward him."

She narrowed her eyes at me. "It's okay, Harley. I won't tell anyone, especially not Jackson. You can trust me. What you say doesn't leave you and me, I promise."

I bit my lip, contemplatin'.

"Come on." She gestured toward the patio. "Let's go where we can have some privacy."

I nodded, followin' behind her. Genuinely curious where she was goin' with this. As soon as we stepped outside, the ocean breeze hit me, blowin' the loose strands of hair away from my heated cheeks. Stirrin' shivers to course up my spine.

"You look beautiful, Harley," she complimented, leaning against the railin', overlookin' the water out on the beach.

"Thank you, so do you."

She smiled, bumpin' her shoulder into mine. "I saw you guys dancing earlier. What happened?"

"Nothin'."

"This isn't going to work unless you're honest with me."

I sighed, takin' a deep breath. "I don't know. He's just so confusin'."

"In the very best way, right?"

"You're jokin'?"

"Yes," she chuckled. "Jackson is anything but easy to understand. He's the most complicated boy I've ever met."

"Try knowin' him your entire life."

"I bet."

"It's like I never know where I stand with him. Ya know?"

"I can understand that more than anyone else. He terrorizes me too, Harley."

"Yeah, but at least you know he likes you."

"How exactly?"

"Cuz he does it outta love for you."

"And how does he do it for you?"

"To torture me."

"I see."

"Do you?"

"Yes. I see you're totally in denial over what you mean to him. Harley, outside of his father and Noah, you're his best friend."

I laughed. I couldn't help it. "Now I know you gotta be jokin'."

She shook her head. "But I'm not."

"How do ya figure?"

"How do you not? You've been there for him throughout everything. You've written him letters which he keeps in his nightstand."

"How do you know that?"

"I found them one day when I was cleaning up his room. He has a folder with your name on it."

"He does?"

She nodded.

"Why?"

"Because he loves you."

"Oh my God. Now you're usin' the word love?"

"He just doesn't know it. Actually," she thought for a second, "he does. He just doesn't want to admit it out loud. That boy has been devoted to you since I met him."

"I think you might have fallen and hit your head, Camila."

"Jackson shows his love through his antics. It's how he gets your attention."

"You sound like my memaw."

"I know. We've talked about it."

"You have?"

"Yes. All the women in your family know what's up. It's the

men who are blind to it. If your daddy knew how much you meant to him, he'd probably end up in jail for life."

"Wait? What? The women in my family know?"

"Yes. We talk about it often."

"You do?"

"Mmm hmm."

"Whoa."

I looked out at the water, watchin' the waves crash into the shore. Tryin' to reel in everythin' she was tellin' me.

"We were all your age once."

"Let me get this straight. You guys think Jackson is in love with me?"

"Yes... we think you're both in love with each other."

I jerked back. "You think I love him?"

"It's kind of obvious."

"To who?"

"To anyone looking. I mean you spent the last hour staring at him dancing with another girl from across the room."

"That's only cuz Willow's dress is hideous!"

"Harley..."

"What? Did you see what she's wearin'? The girl is so cliché. She has no sense of personal style. I've seen that dress in every store. Like come on, have a little bit of self-expression."

"Is her dress bothering you as much as her having Jackson's attention?"

"A bird can have Jackson's attention, it don't take much."

We laughed.

"Besides... her boobs are all out, so... he's mostly been starin' at those."

"Well, he was staring at yours earlier and most of the night."

For some reason her comment made my heart speed up. "He was?"

"Do you know he has videos and photos of you on his phone?"

My eyes widened. "You've seen them?"

"I've seen him staring at them. A lot."

"Are we talkin' about the same Jackson?"

"The pain in the ass that is now officially my son? Yes, that one."

203

"I heard about that. Congratulations, and I'm sorry."

She giggled. "I love Jackson. He's very much like his father. Stubborn, always has to be right, but loves with his whole heart and soul. You're very lucky to have him."

"His mom used to say that to me all the time."

Bailey was constantly reminding me how much Jackson cared for me in one way or another. I still remembered the last time I spoke to her before she lost it completely.

It was the best and worst day of my life. Yet, here I was four years later.

Still waiting for the right time to—

"She was a very smart woman," Camila interrupted my train of thought.

"Aunt Bailey was the best."

"Willow doesn't mean anything to Jackson."

"I doubt that."

"She doesn't, Harley. Boys will be boys, and he is no different."

"They're together a lot."

"Only because she's over for Journey, but he doesn't care about her like he does you."

"That's exactly it, Camila. I never know where I stand with him. One day I feel like he hates me, then the next, I feel like I maybe gettin' somewhere with him. And then we're back to square one."

"Do you love him?"

I shrugged. "I don't know."

"Yes, you do."

"Do I care for him? Of course, I do. He's my family. Other than that, it's all very confusin'. Sometimes I see these moments in him where he's so real… like that wall he's built comes down a little and he lets me in, and then when he realizes he did… he pushes me away again. I wanted to be his friend. Especially that night when his dad hit him, but he was so cruel. After that night, I just couldn't deal with his bs anymore. It's exhaustin'. He's exhaustin'."

"Most men are, honey."

The music from the reception picked up, thumpin' through the windows that lined the back of the buildin'. I wanted to turn around and search for Jackson, but I willed myself to stay put.

"I want a guy who wants to be with me. The one who will do anythin' to make me happy. The man who puts me first before everythin' and anyone. I want the fairytale, my own Prince Charmin'. I know my worth, and I won't stop till I find him. I refuse to settle. It's just not in me."

"That's beautiful, sweetheart. Most girls your age don't realize that until they're much older."

"I don't think Jackson would ever put my needs and wants before his. He's too selfish."

"I think he already has in ways you can't see yet."

"Like how?"

"I can't point them out for you, Harley. It's something you need to realize on your own. What I can tell you is you have his heart. I've known that since the first time I met you. The way he looks at you, the way you make him laugh and smile, the way he watches you when he knows you're not looking. You have that boy wrapped around your finger, babe."

"You think?"

"I know."

I smiled. I couldn't help that either.

Maybe she was right.

"There you are, my tiny dancer," Uncle Aiden chimed in, comin' up behind her. He wrapped his arms around her neck, pullin' her closer to him. "Harley, that's quite a dress."

"Thanks, I made it myself."

"What are you two doing out here?"

"Talkin' about your son," I replied for her. Trustin' him.

"I see."

"Do you think Jackson loves me?'

"Of course, he does. What's not to love?"

"You're supposed to say that."

He smiled, remindin' me of his boy.

"When you were first born, Bailey was already planning your wedding."

"I know. She used to tell me all about it."

He kissed the top of Camila's head. "My boy is a shit, Harley. You know that more than anyone else."

"Yeah."

"Have you seen him by any chance?"

"I haven't."

I wanted them to enjoy the rest of their night. This wasn't about me. It was their wedding, and I didn't want them to remember the whiny girl who took up their time.

"Okay, I'll leave you two alone. Congratulations again."

They smiled, embracin' one another before I turned and left. Goin' to find the boy who confused me the most.

Grabbin' my purse from the back of my chair, I went around lookin' for him.

"Have you seen Jackson?" I asked Jagger, who was standin' by Cash.

He shook his head no.

"Last time I saw him he was goin' down to the beach," Cash answered, noddin' behind me toward the direction I just came from. "Why you lookin' for him?"

"No reason."

"Cash, you dance wif me!" Journey intervened, grabbin' his hands.

"I danced with you five times already."

"Again," she giggled, lookin' up at him like he was her everythin'. Makin' all of us laugh.

"Okay. Let's go dance."

She beamed as he led her toward the dance floor. Once they were there, he twirled her around, and then placed her on his shoes.

I watched them dance, while I talked to Jagger for a bit. Only thinkin' about Jackson Pierce. We laughed our asses off when Shiloh threw a drink in Trigger's face.

"What's that about?"

"Who knows with them. I'm gonna go look for your brother."

"Good luck."

Ten minutes later and still no sign of him. I decided to go toward the pier instead, knowin' it was one of his favorite spots. Takin' off my heels, I made my way in that direction.

What would I say to him when I found him?

Should I tell him what Camila and I talked about?

Would he be receptive?

Push me away?

Be mean to me?

Should I give him what I always carried with me in my purse?

The list of questions was never ending.

I rounded the corner, seein' him up ahead.

There he is!

Rushin' toward him, I was about to call out his name, when I abruptly stopped dead in my tracks. All the blood drained from my face, and my stomach dropped to the sand.

My heart.

My mind.

My love…

Was broken.

Snappin' like a wrought iron chain. He was pullin' every sentiment from my body, every last emotion I didn't even know I had for him.

I strained, lockin' up, stayin' firmly rooted to the place I stood with the wind knocked out of me. Feelin' as though he'd just punched me in the stomach.

Instantly, wantin' to throw up.

I gasped for my next breath at the exact second, he peered up, mid thrust. Connectin' eyes with me while he fucked Willow under the pier on the beach.

"Fuck…" he rasped, realizin' I caught him with her.

Our eyes never wavered from one another, as I realized what I'd truly interrupted.

I winced at the sound of his voice, and for a moment, my pain broke through the uncontrollable emotions.

"Jackson, what the hell?" Willow accused as he stood, tuckin' himself back into his pants.

"You fuckin' liar!" I seethed, feelin' fury and agony like I'd never felt in my life. Before he could humiliate me further, I took off runnin'.

"Harley!" he shouted, chasin' after me.

Only addin' gasoline to my furious, out of control, fiery blaze.

My feet pounded against the sand, kickin' up dirt. I'd never run so fast in my entire life. I didn't want to talk to him, see him, answer to him.

He deserved none of it.

"Harley, stop running!"

His request only had me sprintin' faster. I should have known better, there was no way I'd be able to outrun him. He did this every day of his life for football.

In two seconds flat, I felt his hand firmly grasp my arm. Tearin' me back to face him.

"You fuckin' liar!" I yelled, tryin' to knee him in the balls to get away from him, but with no luck.

He blocked me.

"For fuck's sake, relax!" he ordered, assaultin' me with his whiskey breath.

They were drinkin'?

"You disgust me! I can't believe you! Just two hours ago, you were tellin' me you were a virgin and wanted to save it for someone special!"

"I didn't say that."

"Yes, you did!"

"Harley, don't put words in my mouth. I didn't mean it like that."

"Fine! Then let me go!"

"I didn't mean to hurt you."

"You didn't hurt me!" I lied, not wantin' him to think I gave a shit about him or the pain he caused me. "I fuckin' hate you!"

"It's not what you think."

"Really? Cuz it sure as shit looked like you were fuckin' her!"

"I was."

"Ugh! Let go of me!"

"It was just a fuck! What's your problem?"

"Fuck you!"

"What? You gonna go find Cash now, baby girl?"

"Leave him out of this! This has nothin' to do with him!"

"That's where you're wrong."

I ripped my arms out of his strong grip, speakin' with conviction. "I fuckin' hate you. I believed you. I wanted to believe you. I thought..." I shook my head, holdin' back the tears. "I mean... I just thought... you were talkin' about me in there..."

He frowned, feelin' the sting of my declaration. Stumblin' back.

"I never wanna speak to you again. If you come near me, I swear I'll tell my father anythin' to make you go away for good. I hope she was worth it, cuz you've lost me. Your fuckin' play toy!" I grabbed the envelope out of my purse. "Remember your question on the roof after your mom's funeral? What else had your mom given me? Well, here's your answer. She gave me this before she died. She said I was the only one she trusted to give it to you when the time was right. But I never plan to speak to you again! So here you go, asshole!"

"The fuck?" he breathed out, confused.

Now or never, Harley. Give it to him.

I slapped it against his chest.

"Here are the results of your DNA Dementia test. Have a nice life."

TO BE CONTINUED...

The continuation of the Love Hurts Duet
Love You Now

Made in the USA
Columbia, SC
02 October 2021